CA

Aphid & The Shadow Drinkers
ಬೋ

Aphid
&
The Shadow Drinkers
ఇఒ

Steven Lattey

THISTLEDOWN PRESS

© Steven Lattey, 1999
All rights reserved

No part of this publication may be reproduced or transmitted in any form or by any means, graphic, electronic or mechanical, including photocopying, recording, or any information storage and retrieval system, without permission in writing from the publisher.

Canadian Cataloguing in Publication Data

Lattey, Steve.
Aphid & the shadow drinkers
ISBN 1-895449-93-6
I. Title.
PS8573.A7793A75 1999   C813'.54   C99-920116-6
PR9199.3.L3282A75 1999

Cover painting by Julie Oakes
Typeset by Thistledown Press Ltd.
Printed and bound in Canada

Thistledown Press Ltd.
633 Main Street
Saskatoon, Saskatchewan
S7H 0J8

 Saskatchewan Arts Board

The Canada Council for the Arts since 1957 | Le Conseil des Arts du Canada depuis 1957

 Canadian Heritage   Patrimoine canadien

Thistledown Press gratefully acknowledges the financial assistance of the Canada Council for the Arts, the Saskatchewan Arts Board, and the Government of Canada through the Book Publishing Industry Development Program for its publishing program.

Aphid
&
The Shadow Drinkers

ACKNOWLEDGEMENTS

These stories were first read and critiqued in the literary meetings of the *Kalamalka New Writers*.

Also, the assistance and patience of my loving wife, Carol.

And Seán Virgo, who believed in the stories and pushed for more material. I am most thankful for his keen ear and loving dedication to the art of the story.

Contents

The Shadow Drinkers	9
Jellyface	19
Island Music	29
The Hand of God	41
Heartbreak Hotel	51
The Birth of Faust	61
Behind the Fence	64
Aphid & The Rocket Lawnchair	83
Epilogue	173

The Shadow Drinkers

We had free run of the country, us kids. Fences were meant to climb over and Joe's shack was a regular stop on our boyish wandering. Not like these times when every gate is locked and "No Trespassing" signs are everywhere.

Junky Joe Simard lived in a gully off Pottery Road. The gully was filled with old cars and washing machines and pipes and barrels full of metal junk and in the middle was Joe's tin shack. Joe was a wizened, cave chested, ill shaven, rare bathen, hard drinkin' guy. A bootlegger. A scavenger on his bicycle through town with his cart pulled behind. He hated the sun. He wore too many clothes in the summer and you could only imagine the colour and smell of his skin.

We'd take the trail that led around the rim of the gully, crawl on our bellies through the tall grass to the edge, and fire rocks down onto Joe's shack, glistening in the morning sun. The sound was deafening, even from way up on the bank.

Joe would come running out from inside his tin hut, pulling on his pants and swearing and wheezing up the bank to get at us. He was wonderful in the cruelty of our youth. Our lungs were clean and our skin was smooth. We stood way above him, the sunlight burning his eyes.

We remember Junky Joe Simard because he split away from the other seven brothers. The other Simard brothers stayed in the bush, up in the Shuswap. Henry was the eldest and he came out west, from Quebec, around 1917. He was a communist and he homesteaded a big chunk of land on Shuswap Lake. All the brothers followed him out and they set about logging and raising families and living the communist ideals.

I guess Joe just drifted closer to town to be nearer the customers for his whisky and the junk he collected. And thus, he became a counterweight to our orderly existence. We looked in the mirror to see if Junky Joe was hidden behind our sweet young faces. And he was there, staring back at us, reflecting the dreams we feared the future would steal from us. The future that stretched out in front of us like a night train, howling through the velvet hills, the whistle crying, "promises, promises".

And he reflected the lost dreams of our parents. He was the stark truth of night dragged up into day. Mother and father woke and shed their secrets like a snake's skin in the morning and smiled at the day through polished teeth. Joe woke stinking of whisky. Weeks of whisky.

But today we are walking, my friend Pete and I, with the most pleasant breezes blowing and the range hills across the valley burnt to brown, even during this wet summer. Junky Joe was Pete's great uncle and that's why my mind is turning back to those days when Junky Joe Simard was a famous character in our town. He pushed his bicycle along the maple avenues, the handles comfortably turned

The Shadow Drinkers

up and the large tires equal to the load. One dark eye searching the ditch for junk and one nervous eye peeled for trouble. He roamed the periphery of our little world.

Junky Joe, bless his miserable soul, got beaten to death. The guys that beat him were trying to steal his whisky and they hit him too hard. Joe wasn't very strong from all the drinking and the rough life he had lived so a couple of good smacks is all it took.

That was in 1968, so in a way Joe was lucky to be gone from the world because the world was changing and the days when you could just set up home in an unofficial junkyard and sell bootleg whisky and nobody really gave a damn, well those days were going, going, gone.

The town fathers were busy during those years. They ripped down the granite Government building and the red brick fire hall. They tore the cupola off the top of the post office. In a frenzy they ordered all the big beautiful maple trees that lined the avenues cut down. They were worried about the new times that were coming and they wanted to present a clean, modern image. What they couldn't tear down they covered over.

A new highway through the Selkirk Mountains, east of Revelstoke, had just been completed and cars from the east flooded into town. The air was pungent with the smell of money. Joe's gully became valuable real estate. Guys like Joe weren't needed anymore, to drink down the long dark shadow of our little town. They were like minor gods from some pagan religion, soon forgotten. Junky Joe and the other Shadow Drinkers.

There was Black Santa. He drank down the shadow of our little town for years. Black Santa with gifts far worse than coal in your Christmas stocking. Gifts that blackened more than just fingers. Gifts that could blacken your soul. We didn't throw stones at Black Santa. He was dangerous and we stayed out of his way.

But one day, when I was five years old, I was taking a shortcut on my way to Jocko's house, sliding down the sandy bank and across the tracks, into the neglected lots behind the warehouses. I liked the vacant lots because they were strewn with wrecked cars, sleepy with dust. Black Santa was crawling out of a big, comfortable wreck where he had been sleeping.

He saw me and spat. I circled wide. "C'mere you little motherfucker," he whisky whispered, hoarse but loud. "Listen, you little bastard. I'm gonna tell you someth'n." The perimeter of my circle was limited by a warehouse wall. I was sliding sideways. He fixed me with his red-rimmed eye and waved a crooked finger in my direction. He was lanky and moved with a freaky, off-kiltered agility.

"Yooou listen," he said. "Yooou remember." He was moving forward, spittle frothing in his beard, and I was moving back. "This is all you need to know about women, the bitches, you little fucker, C'mere. I'm gonna tell you." He puffed his chest up ready for his oration, wiped his mouth, and in a fetid blast unleashed this gift upon me, starting in a low growl and each line ascending in pitch and volume. "Yoou find 'em. Yoouu feel 'em. Yooou fuck 'em. And yooouu forget 'em," and he was yelling in a voice like scraping rust from steel and I was running. And then he was laughing and I was gone; but I could imagine him behind me, slapping his knees and dancing around in a drunken pirouette until he collapsed in a fit of coughing. He loved to give his little presents. He was giving back a piece of the shadow that was lodged in his ribcage;

coughing it up and spitting it out at me. *Run! Run!*

Mother said Black Santa had a name once. She said, "His name is Russell Hagy." Mother said this as we drove past the mansion on the hill. "Black Santa once owned that beautiful place," mother said, "all lost to drink." And the words just hung there above the mansion for ever and ever. "All lost to drink," hanging, like a banner, above the huge ponderosa pines.

We were on our way to Terrace Mountain when mother said that. We were going up the mountain to hike and look west into the future. The ponderosa pines shaded the roadway that led to the mansion at the top of hill. We passed in silence to ponder the fate of those who drink the shadow.

Then Mother said, "A good reason to sit up straight at the five o'clock supper, keep your elbows off the table. Brush your teeth."

But nothing could keep away the terrible darkness. The darkness was already inside. I had caught a gift from Black Santa. An angry, lonely gift, like a black stone, lodged between my teeth. The stone was angry speech to name the countless secrets. An angry stone of language to spit out the darkness I had swallowed. Innocently, stupidly, I had swallowed the secrets of others. I had become a shadow drinker.

At night, when the good citizens slept in their beds up on the hill, they exhaled a shadow that, because of its weight, slipped down the hill like a fog. The guys in Hobo Jungle drank whisky and the fog wrapped around their legs and slipped into their cups. They drank down the shadow in big gulps.

The good citizens woke happy in the morning, lighter. They felt as if they walked on air and whistled down the hill to work.

But the simple days were numbered. Soon the jungle would be gone. The hoboes driven out. The shadow drinkers forgotten. And then, the good citizens would have to drink down their own long dark shadow.

The City Park stopped on one side of Okanagan Creek and Hobo Jungle was on the other side. Hobo Jungle was a ragged patch of forest and brush running along the tracks and up under the railway bridge. When we were little we used to go into Hobo Jungle: but only in the daylight. We could imagine the riotous nights around the fire beneath the big cottonwood trees. We found party remnants in the cold black coals and the cold ring of blackened stones and the blackened cans. We sniffed the stinking bottles strewn about and wondered at the bottles smashed . . . in fighting? In laughter? We found places in the dense underbrush where the hoboes had slept on cardboard. You could see the outline of their bodies pressed into the cardboard, like an angel in the snow.

The liquor store was only a half-mile from the Jungle and I slept safely in my child's bed, up on the hill, just a breath away from the Jungle. The ordered world spun so close.

The Jungle was ripped out after the little paper boy was found raped and murdered in the bushes. The town was in an uproar and the forest was cleared out. Everyone was happy to see it go. They had only been waiting for an excuse.

A few years later, the boy's father drank himself to death in the park. He slept behind the bushes across the creek from where his little boy had died. He drank down the saddest of shadows.

At that time I worked in the park as a gardener and would see the boy's father in the morning, shaking in the gazebo, waiting for the liquor store to open. He would ask me for a buck to make up the price of a bottle and I always said "yes". I figured, "What the fuck?" I am still haunted by his pale blue eyes, even though these ugly crimes have become so common now. I still think of that little paper boy selling Kelowna Couriers on the street in front of the Kalamalka Hotel. When I walk past the house where he lived I feel the shadows of the father, who was a mechanic before he was an alcoholic, and the little paper boy, hovering over the house. Or only in my mind?

But that day, we were driving to Terrace Mountain, we were driving past Black Santa's lost mansion. That day, the memory is like a bubble. We were little. We were in the back seat. Daddy was driving and Mother was being very careful so we would not slip behind her eyes and see the dreaming fields where death, fear of death and the smell of death clung to every blade and branch. Mommy has a secret. Daddy keeps the secret for Mommy. And he keeps his own secrets too. But Mommy's secret is much worse. See how the secrets pile up?

Mother turns from the front seat to straighten hair and wipe noses. "You will not know. You will not know, my beautiful children," she whispers to herself. But Mother's secret is following us everywhere we go. Especially when the wheels in the car are spinning around and making that flat sound on the road.

That is a sound the secret likes to follow, slouching along

behind us or waiting around the bend, leaning against a fence rail. His hat pulled down over his eyes. A sneer his salient feature. He is a nasty, impudent secret.

"I belong to you," he says to me and raises his hand to his hat, in a blurred salute, as we speed by.

"You are mine," he says to me, guttural and foreign, and his voice is lost in the flat whir of wheels.

We did not know who the secret was. How could we? We were little and learning to count. We knew we had ten toes. We knew that girls were different from boys. But we did not know who the secret was. The secret did not say "Good day" like every one else. The secret said, *Guten Tag*" like Mrs. Hoofnagel on the doorstep. Knock knock with her *apfel kuchen* and her braided bread, her strudels, her stollens and her poppy-seed cakes. Oh *ya, mein gott*, they had suffered.

And the secret was hidden in the language. But the meaning ran away and hid in the bushes. Nobody is telling us kids anything.

Mrs. Hoofnagel, Elmgart and Gert and their babies, the seven Knittels, old to young, all standing on the doorstep. And mother stands in the door. She is the gateway to this new country.

"*Wie Geht's, Wellkommen,*" she says in her perfect High German and,

"How do you do?" in her perfect English. "Forget the past," she says,

"We are all Germans in a new country. And things are tough."

They all carry bundles of secrets over their shoulders and they trudge up the steps and they lay the bundles down in

The Shadow Drinkers

the backyard. "I am too little," I moan. And I cry and cry waking from my afternoon nap. All cranky. I do not want to drink this shadow. I am too young and this is too horrible.

When I wake from my nap, I am ill because of bad dreams I cannot understand. "Why do they bring them here?" I ask mother and I point to the bags of secrets strewn on the lawn. "You are a silly boy," she says and strokes the hair from my face. "There are no bags of secrets on the lawn, you are a silly boy."

But I have seen the secrets in my dreams escaping from the bags, hissing across the lawn and swirling around my bed.

Mother's secret was not even her own secret. The secret had been sown inside her belly when she was asleep. When she was a little girl. Her father was a surgeon and he performed the operation himself. She was a good girl and didn't complain. The secret slept when she slept and turned when she turned. There was nothing she could do. The secret had saved her life so she was stuck with it.

"Look. Look," Mother said. "Outside all beautiful and blue. The mountains. The peace. There is no secret. It is only your imagination."

But when Mother slept her secret slipped down the hill with all the other shadows and nobody could drink it down. They vomited on the ground from the stench. The meanest hobo of them all cried, "I am too innocent to drink this vile shit." He drank anyway, to prove some point, and died. Mother's secret.

But that day, driving past Black Santa's lost estate, we were on a pilgrimage to the top of Terrace Mountain to visit the man at the forestry lookout. We went up very steep. The road had deep ruts and the tires spun throwing showers of rocks down the cliff. We had driven as far as we could in the powder blue '55 Chevrolet.

We walked up the last pitch, father carrying the rucksack full of food. We ran around in the meadows on the mountain top and put our arms up to the elbows in the cold little lakes. We stood in the wind and looked west over the miles of scrub pine. In the distance we could see open ranges. And beyond the open ranges a line of big mountains. And beyond the mountains there were rumours of a big city and an ocean. We didn't know we were looking into the future. How could we?

We ate our lunch behind a rock, out of the wind. Pickle and tongue sandwiches on dark bread. Honey sandwiches and hard-boiled eggs. Smelly cheese and apples. Dark chocolate. All wrapped in waxed paper and passed around from father's rucksack. We looked down into the shimmering warm blue of our valley shrouded in the smoke of summer fires. The entire known world, stretching out in darkening shades, at our feet.

For the first time, we were outside looking in. The wind whipped over the rock and around our heads and Mother and Father pointed out the landmarks below. Then Mother said,

"The secret can not follow us here, on the mountain top."

"Because the air is too thin," Father said, putting his arm around her shoulder.

"And here, in the alpine meadows," Mother said, "everyone is a foreigner."

Jellyface

It's a full day walk from my cabin, at the edge of the forest, to the place where I can see across the badlands. That's where the trouble's coming from. I can stand on the soft earth, at the cliff's edge, and look out across that baked and cracked stretch of dog-dung desert we call, simply, the flats. I can stand here on this lush meadow, in the spring sun, with my back to the forest and the hill and wait for those bastards. I'm happy waiting and watching. It's spring and I'm laughing inside all the time and every breath I take makes me feel strong.

I have a fat baby and a woman, Lenora, with skin so pale and soft and hair so black she is like a beautiful wisp of white smoke. They are back in the little cabin waiting for me. When I go to the cliff, I leave before daylight and don't return until late at night. Behind the cabin a thickly wooded hillside rises steeply to the ridge.

These two men that are coming smell very bad. One is my Lenora's brother; the other one is her husband. These guys have been dogging my trail across the centuries. They always smelled bad, even in that East European Country where they had me cornered.

They got me in my mishaped body with its knobbled knees, its drooling lip, its withered arm. They took me up the hill above that bleak little village. They took me right in front of that big, fat, greasy woman with the dirty apron who says she's my mother. They grabbed me by the arms and marched me up the steep hill over the cobblestones, between the grey, high faces of dirty little flats stacked on top of each other; past the place where the cobblestones end and the stony path begins. I can feel the stones through the hole in my second-hand shoe. And my pants are ripped, my precious blue pants. And my white shirt, saved for some special day, is soiled.

They take me to the top of the hill and drag me through the iron gates into the cemetery. Near the gate there is a mausoleum where the town's noble family is buried and there is a big old tree near the door of this mausoleum. I am so scared I can't breathe. They string me up in this tree, by the arms, and slit my belly open so my guts spill out. I die turning in the wind with my toes pointed together. The year is 1762 and I am only 14 years old.

And now they are coming again, a hundred years later. But I am happy inside myself, waiting, because I am big now. I am a big man with power pulsing from my solar plexus and a dark blue cape thrown over my right shoulder and my little rifle slung across my back. I have a chest like a barrel and my hands are so large they are like hams. My face is very round and fleshy and pockmarked and I have jowls that hang down and my whole face moves around like a bowl of jelly when I walk. My eyes laugh out at the world through folds of fat. I'm a big, ugly Indian. They call me Jellyface.

✦ ✦ ✦

Jellyface

I was the village idiot back in that East European Country. I was a slave to that horrible woman but she said I was her son. I couldn't talk properly and my body was all wrong. I was weak and sickly and twisted like a plant grown in the dark. I can remember sitting on the floor while she worked on a big table, in front of a dirty little window, at the end of a long, dark, attic room, rolling and pounding dough. She was the baker for the village. She wore her dark, filthy hair pulled back tight against her head. She would throw me raw dough to eat. She threw it down on the never-washed plank floor, in the dirt and grease. I would sneak out from my dark corner, grab the slimy morsel, and scurry back. I tried to clean the dough against my dirty pants.

Then I would go outside and walk around and try not to let anyone see me. I wasn't allowed to go to school. They said I was too stupid, but I could read and count and add and subtract. I could not speak though, and slobbered down my chin.

Those boys belonged to some kind of military youth club. They didn't actually carry guns yet, because they are too young, but they had leather straps over their shoulders; they are half-way ready. They are practising on me. They call it playing. They come into the house and tell Mother, Magda, they want to take me out to play. I run and hide but she finds me and shoves me out the door. She knows they beat me but she says I am clumsy and fall down, which is true: I am clumsy.

They push me down the hill that runs above the river to the east of town and then they rescue me, dragging me up the rocky bank and through the spindly forest of yellow trees that grows along the top of the bank. We play war and they hit me with sticks and take me prisoner. They torture me to make me tell secrets. I don't know any secret so they hit me again.

I call this country, this life, "The Narrow Place". There is no room here. The people smell awful and stand too close and there is always something bad going on. There is always somebody whispering in the corner. There are men marching through the streets in the night and the sound of their boots on the cobblestones echoes between the rows of flats.

Those two boys strung me up by the arms, ripped open my shirt, laughed at my scrawny chest and swollen stomach, slit my belly and left me to die slow and painful. My guts drying in the open air. My feet inches above the ground. I died and I left that narrow place and came here, to a country with open space. I floated down from the sky like a leaf falling off a tree and I could see miles and miles of rolling hills covered in tall grass. I grew strong here, in a big country of hills and forests and canyons and deserts. And now I stand and wait to meet those two guys again.

✦ ✦ ✦

I watched all spring and summer from my place on the cliff and I built a little log house at the edge of the meadows, with our back against the forest and the hill. In the fall I did some hunting but I never wandered so far that I couldn't walk out across that rolling meadow, with little groves of aspen here and there, to the place on the cliff where I can see east across the desert flats.

The east horizon is a low line of desert mountains. Hot,

Jellyface

barren, piles of rock. A man riding west comes out of those mountains onto the desert; two days ride with not even a rock for shade. A baked and cracked ancient salt sea bottom. The cactus don't even like being out there. They crowd around the edges of the desert and thin out like brave soldiers toward the centre, to nothing.

These two men are coming from the east. They come from a big cattle ranch beyond the barren mountains, on the rich prairie. I was working at that place for a while. Lenora's father owned the ranch and her brother was lead-hand. I slept in the barn and Lenora would come and see me and I would hold her close and tell her not to be scared. She was like a bird shivering in my hand. Her husband was a mean bastard. He beat her when he drank and he was cold-hearted when he was sober, so Lenora and I ran away together. I was laughing the night we sneaked off, thinking about the commotion we left behind. Her father would make those guys come after me. Lenora was the apple of his eye and she had run off with a big, ugly savage. There would be hell to pay.

I had been away from my own country too long. Scouting for the army. Fighting for pay. Working for white men. I was tired of that life. I was taking this woman I loved back home.

I watched for those guys all fall, and the winter came. We had fresh meat, some flour, some coffee. And I had that woman, Lenora, who took my breath away — she moved like a willow in the wind.

The first storms of winter were ferocious. The snow piling up in the mountains and blowing in big drifts across the flats. I walked out to my lookout on the cliff and watched out for those two guys every second day, no matter the weather, and, finally, I saw them crossing round the north rim of the flats. They were no bigger than fleas weaving their way through the rock pillars, the hoodoos, that stood sentinel along the northern boundary of the desert.

When I saw those guys I went crazy, dancing on that cliff. My spirit crouched low and sprang in a war leap, high above the desert. Then I danced slow on the earth, lifting my legs with care and treading lightly. I sang a song to announce my intention that I would kill these men. I sang my song into the rocks, into the trees, into the cold earth where their blood would seep. Every winter bird cocked its head against the howling wind, to hear this song they understood without reason. Every animal stopped and listened and the resounding "YES" shot through my body in a ripple of power and joy. My chest pounded hard enough to break my ribs. My step was light and certain.

Those two guys: Lenora's pretty blonde husband with the cruel, narrow, too-red mouth and her swarthy and corpulent brother with the little red eyes of a pig. Those two guys thought they could sneak across the desert through the windblown rock pillars and then up the valley that opened wide off the flats.

The valley is the only break in an unbroken line of cliff stretching south along the west edge of the desert as far as the eye can see. They didn't know the wide mouth of the valley narrowed quickly into the box canyon and the only way up the steep south slope of that canyon, to my little cabin, was a willow-choked nightmare.

As a rider enters the valley he notices the south slope rising up the ridge is steep, loose, rock slides. He pushes farther on and the valley becomes narrow and the slope to the ridge becomes sand cliffs, impossible to climb. A little farther up the valley, he rides into a box canyon, horse hooves ringing echoes on the stone floor. The rider remembers a creek gully rising steeply to the ridge about two hours ride back down the canyon. The creek is so little, and the water in such great demand, it is dry before it reaches the canyon floor, but in its wake is a strangle of willow brush. The little creek is the only way up the ridge and up the ridge is the only way to me.

My grandfather brought me to this country when I was a little boy, about 10 years old. We came across the desert from way south, maybe a hundred miles, where there is a single steep trail that rises off the desert, up the cliff and onto The Meadow With Many Streams. I was riding a roan mare with a broad back. The mare was so gentle I could sleep on her and she would never let me fall.

We camped on the meadow beside the many streams and my grandfather showed me the country and drew maps with a stick in the sandy banks so I would never forget this place. He drew The Hot Mountains to the east, The Dog Shit Desert and The Long Cliff on the west side of the desert. He drew The Meadow With Many Streams on top of The Long Cliff. West and north of the meadow he drew the steep Wooded Hills. And farther north, down the backside of The Wooded Hills, he drew The Trap Canyon. He told me my life would be full of trouble. He told me to come here and I would be safe. He said I could fight against a whole army from this Great Natural Fortress. And there was always lots of game.

I get tears in my eyes when I remember my grandfather. He was so kind to me even though I was damn ugly. He would say,

"You can kill your enemy with that ugly face,"
And I would jump around, yelling, and make my face shake like jelly and my eyes pop out and we would both laugh. He named me Jellyface. He made me proud to be so ugly. I got my bad sense of humour from my grandfather.

I didn't even bother to watch those two guys after they left the flats. They would be three days up the willow-choked creek bed in the deep snow. My little willow friends would slap their faces every step of the way.

On the afternoon of the third day they would be on top of the ridge behind my little cabin.

I went out on the afternoon of the third day with my rifle and my knife. My blue cloak and buckskin trousers. I had some food and warm moccasins with high leggings. I made myself comfortable in the snow with my rifle across my lap and my cape around me. I disappeared inside myself. The power from my chest was so strong I was warm all over. The winter was nothing to me!

Just before dark they were coming close. It was snowing hard and the wind blew the snow sideways. I could hear their leather saddles creaking as they came down the steep trail from the ridge. I could smell the whisky and the heavy rotten hides they wore as coats. I would kill them because they were so heavy in their coats and I was so light.

Their smell had soured over the centuries. Back in that other country, that European Country, they had smelled of the sickly-sweet sweat of pubescent perverts covered with splashes of lavender cologne. Now, a century later, their smell was almost solid; the rot was so far gone. Their smell hit me like a dog smelling a snake. The dog's head, when he catches the snake scent, snaps back like he's been kicked in the chops. Their smell was that bad.

The first guy coming down the hill was the fat one, Lenora's brother. I stepped out from behind the big birch tree, dressed light as a feather, shirtless, my cloak lying on the snow behind me. Lenora's brother was slightly below me, moving down the hill from left to right, his horse up to her belly in the snow. He turned in the saddle at my movement. We exchanged "a look" and I shot him in the side: right between the ribs. I can still see the exact spot where the bullet went in.

I jumped the blonde one, Lenora's husband, and killed him with my knife. I preferred to kill him with my hands. I meant to shoot him but I was overcome with passion and dropped my gun, jumped over the bank, knocked him to the ground and slit his throat. I held his long blonde hair and sliced his scalp. He gurgled and, in his conceit, looked surprised. He had been so sure of himself.

Now, there are two graves up on the hill and there is one fat Indian, with a face like a bowl of jelly, down in the cabin eating bannock and eggs. I'm one lucky man and I have two fine horses, saddles and all.

I wanted to leave their bodies for the animals to eat the flesh and scatter the bones but Lenora made me string them up in a tree. In the spring she wanted me to bury them but I pretended I couldn't find them. I ran around the little cabin looking under the bed and in the corners, making a big joke. I pretended my back was too sore to dig the hole. I made a big show and moaned and groaned. I pretended I couldn't find the shovel. But Lenora got mad, so I buried them.

I left her brother's big stinking fur coat hanging on a tree for a while just so I could look at the hole where the bullet went through and the dry blood matted the dark fur. It made me happy to look at that coat but Lenora made me take it down. She said, "After all, he was my brother."

So I took the baby and held him up and showed him the hole where his daddy shot a bad man. The baby put his finger in the hole and that made me laugh all afternoon.

Island Music

The day before the wedding the bride was sullen. Tight lipped, arms crossed. She was angry at the groom. He had been out the night before and he had promised two young fellows he met in a bar a ride north, up the coast. The bride decided the two fellows might be dangerous and slash her throat. The groom laughed and that made her even more angry.

He regretted his laughter and tried reason. "Look at them," he said pointing to the myopic boy, too thin, phoning home to mother for replacement glasses (lost in the surf). And his shy friend, a Carolina farm boy who, no matter what he was doing, seemed to be picking his teeth with a piece of straw. They were just like he was when he was that age. Looking for the place where your own life begins.

The groom wanted to give his bohemian past a little ride up the coast. He wanted to give these young guys the courtesy he would have appreciated. They were just young guys out looking for their place. Not a dangerous bone in their bodies.

It felt important he give these boys a ride. Especially

now that he was to be married. Marriage seemed like a time to honour his past. Embrace and be reconciled to his past. And so he must give these two boys a ride. He must. The bride felt it was important to object. Loudly and with jutted jaw.

Bad things were said on both sides. He rued the day he met her and her uptight shit and he said so. She rose high on her righteous horse. How dare he endanger her life? She said. She'd been taught a different sort of behaviour, not brought up like this, to pick up strangers in the bar.

They had met in a bar themselves, danced, made love the first night. But she was too busy enjoying her anger to notice the inconsistency. Despite her wrath he insisted on giving the two fellows a ride. They drove to pick up the boys at an outdoor cafe. She sat on the bench in the warm morning sun waiting for her throat to be slit and the boys said no they would not need a ride, thankyou. They would wait for the glasses to be sent from the mother, thankyou. They were such polite young fellows. So the two of them, the man and the woman, went on alone, up the coast.

The fight of words was over and the silence follows. The deadly silence of couples fighting. Stalemate. No one moves. A pin could drop. Muscles are tense. She rustles the map. He coughs and points. They drive north and the land begins to seep into their pores. They drive north through the black desolation of lava. They begin to be curious, not understanding where they have landed but sensing something powerful. The heat nibbles at the edge of their anger. Neck muscles fight to stay tense but are unable to sustain under attack from all the senses. A drowsiness overcomes them. Something is touching their faces, like feathers. They drive north, arms out the

Island Music

windows. The moist smell of thousands of flowers up the road, ahead of them.

As they drive north along the coast there are small beaches, coves where palm trees and sand crouch like an oasis on the coastal edge of the harsh lava flows. These are pockets of life the destruction has spared, has flowed around and missed. Between these coves the magma has flowed right into the ocean and the land supports a rugged and stunted vegetation. They must be hardy plants to survive. There is little water on this side of the island and there is no soil, only crumbling volcanic rock.

The bride and groom stop and swim at the little beaches as they travel north through the hot scrub that grows on the lava. They plunge in water that startles for only a moment and then soothes. They stop at a roadside attraction. An historical site.

In a small building there is a map on the wall and a woman with a pointer. She has a uniform and she is paid by the government but she was hired because she knows the history of this place. The woman is very efficient. She speaks quickly about the stones piled up. The stones were brought out of the water by thousands of workers who lived on the hillside. She says. The stones were carried up the hill and piled into a structure thirty feet high and one hundred feet long and fifty feet wide. The landscape is intersected by stone fences that radiate from the structure. She speaks quickly. The man asks about the sacrifices but the woman is evasive. The other tourists leave the building and walk down the hill to the great kings' sacrificial altar. The bride leaves the room because she feels the woman is hostile. The man is asking too many questions. Killing people is a delicate subject.

The groom keeps asking questions of the woman with the stick. It is a talking stick and, because she holds it, the woman must answer the questions. She looks at this guy who is asking so damn many questions and the stick in her hand starts talking. She doesn't want to speak but she can't stop the words from pouring out of her mouth. Her dark eyes are firm. They are hard and black, like lava. She says,

"You be careful what you say with your mouth, and even what you think with your mind because your words and your thoughts go out like electricity into the air." It is as if she knows about the fight and all the bad words spoken. She says,

"In our language the greatest word is the word "HA". HA is electricity in the air. Every breath we take we breathe in HA and that is the power of life." The great word is the core of their language and religion. She says.

"You do whatever you want with this great gift. This HA. You can be depressed all day if you want. You do whatever you want because you are MAN and you have freedom of will." Then she said,

"The rest of the animals they follow the rule of nature but not man. He makes his own rules. He makes his own decisions."

The bride was impatient and came inside and tugged at the groom's sleeve and they walked down the hill to the historical monument. The man walked out into the sunlight in a daze, as though he had been hit on the forehead with that talking stick. He was a stranger in that land and didn't know about talking sticks.

Later he would get a glimpse. Later he would see the

last King's talking stick lying against the trunk of a tree, whitened with age. Lying where the King had left it one hundred and fifty years ago. He would see the King's canoe lying nearby. The sides broken down and the bottom split nearly in two, but the carved prow still rising proudly to the sky. He would see the King's carved god, his Tiki, lying carelessly on top of a stone wall and the tall carved post, to the God Lono, lying as if it were cast away behind the wall. There were offerings on the canoe wrapped in leaves. But that would come later. Later they would find that place. Find that place like a lesson, right beneath their feet. Laugh together at their mutual blindness. Laugh together at the way the clues had been so obvious. There it would be, behind the swimming pool of the hotel. A shrine. A temple.

The bride and groom walked down the hill to the historical monument. The structure, if judged by size, or architecture, or complexity of design, was not so marvelous. If judged by the intellect, then this thing was nothing. There were no arches. No pillars. No finely wrought angels in marble. There were only these rocks piled up in this dry place where the grasses, the bushes and the stunted trees grow on the lava.

But some other effect was on this place. When asked about the sacrifices The Woman With The Stick said the chiefs were not killed in this place. They were brought here after they were vanquished, she said. And that is all she said. And then what? What was done after they were vanquished? What was done on the flat top of this huge altar?

The man stared up at the squat structure that hugged the earth. Electricity shivered his spine and stole his breath.

The woman held his arm tightly, suddenly afraid. There was blood spilt here. He could smell it on the rocks. The woman said, "I would not touch a stone in this place." The man trembled, feeling the edge of a knife running down his spine. The sky turned hot and dark. A wind came up and a few drops of rain fell.

Looking back, the syncopation had begun the first morning; as if the land were eager to respond; could feel them treading overhead. The ground on this island is very thin and hollow. Fire beneath your feet, pockets of air. Huge caverns running hot and cold to the centre of the earth. A labyrinth of volcanic channels that push up, at various times and places all around the island. Small volcanoes, mere mounds, and huge mother volcanoes. Small calderas, puckered explosions a few meters in diameter spitting their magma to the sky. And huge calderas, perfectly round, with cliffs four hundred feet high and in the pit, miles and miles of desolation with steam rising through the cracked lava rock. Put your ear to the earth and listen to the rivers of fire flowing up to greet you.

The groom had woken early, on the first morning, and walked out of their room and across the grounds. He walked through a tidal pool and along the shore toward a deserted building. He sat on the sand in front of the fence. There was a young boy on the beach and the man asked the boy about the place. "That is the bankrupt hotel," the boy said. The night watchman came by with his morning cup of coffee.

The night watchman was happy to have people to talk with after the long dark night. "For hundreds of years this was all a graveyard," he said, nodding toward the shattered windows and blistered paint. "They didn't take all the bones out of the ground." He said, "Maybe there are still bones under the building. Maybe that's why they didn't make any money?" He took a sip of coffee from the styrofoam cup and the three of them looked through the high wire fence into the desolate swimming pool and the ragged grounds strewn with storm-broken branches, husks and rotting fruits.

"There are big cracks in the walls," the night watchman continued. "Not here, but around back of the building, near the long house." The long house was a building on the hotel grounds used for banquets and feasts by the royal family, long ago, before they were overthrown, before there was any hotel. "If you dug down below the crack in the wall you would find the bones of a King or Priest. The bones of a King are strong enough to break concrete," the night watchman said with authority.

Here he paused to sip some coffee and drink the joyful light of morning before he plunged into the darkness that was the soul of this place. "I have seen something in the long house," said the night watchman, "something out of the corner of my eye. If you look straight at the thing, it's gone." He gestured with his hand like a bird flying away. "But I could see it out of the corner of my eye, white and shimmering. It was something small, like a child."

He paused once more and breathed deeply as though to draw into himself the endless blue horizon and dispel the night air that clung to his lungs. He continued, "When the hotel was still in business there was a child killed around back, near the long house. They had a Tiki there, a statue, just like the one that stands behind the hotel where you are staying," and the night watchman nodded gravely to the man. "The child was playing near the Tiki and the

Tiki fell over and crushed her. She was a twin child. A little girl. I know the family." And he mentioned the name of the family of the killed child and the big boy said yes, yes he had heard the name.

The groom went back to his hotel and slipped into bed with the woman. Her skin smelt of the ocean. She awoke from the intensity of island dreams to the rhythmic sound of waves. Moist breezes. Gentle sucking kisses. That was the first morning. There were loving gifts, luscious fruits from the land and sea, all senses expanding. And there, on the first morning, was the white hotel, empty, desolate and somehow holy. A shrine to the retribution of bones. A cursed place. And Salvador, the night watchman, singing the first few threads of island music.

Every night the dreams were intense. The arguments went around and round in the groom's chest, like a whirlwind of insects. The arguments were with people he wanted to leave behind. This was to be a new beginning, on this island, but in the dreams the people did not want to leave. They wanted to stay and buzz around in his chest forever. In the dreams he pointed at different doors for the arguing people to leave through. They would go out that door and come right back through another, on the other side of the circle. The dreams left a knot the size of a baseball in the centre of his chest. He woke from the dreams in the middle of the night and listened to the surf on the shore. With all of the buzzing in his chest he thought he would choke in this paradise.

The bride dreamed she was ordered about by friends, scolded, chided, bossed around. And she dreamed of sexual encounters with military personnel pressing against her, front and back. She fought against their strength but the land and sea were merciless, there was no place to turn. She was dragged down into dream, lulled by scent, drugged with heat. She was lost. She was drowning with every breath.

So each night, for several nights, they fought a losing battle against the sensual earth. They slept restlessly in their separate dreams, unable to hear each other's cries. During the days they explored the island.

They stopped at a small cafe and had a simple lunch of rice and fish. They were paying at the counter and there was an old man sitting on a stool by the cash register eating lunch. Beside his plate there were a half dozen dead flies. The old man said, "See, I lay them on the counter so I can count how many I kill." He laughed. The groom asked him if he could grab them out of the air with one hand. The old man said, "No, I get them like this," and he clapped his hands together. The groom said, "You're a better man than me. I can never get them no matter which way I try." The old man laughed again and said, "You gotta get them when they close their eyes." The groom laughed and said, "A fly has thousands of eyes. When does he have them all closed?" And they both laughed thinking of all those eyes open, and then closed. And the fast hands of the old man. That seemed to get rid of all the arguments that were buzzing around in the groom's chest. The pain in his chest just disintegrated with the laughter. Those arguments were dead.

They travelled south from the little town with the cafe to a beach where the sand was black and flecked with green. They met a man named Koumaka who lived on the beach. He was standing on the lava rock looking over his bay. Long white hair, feet well planted on the ground.

Smoking a cigarette.

This black sand beach. This bay with turtles is the place he was born and the place he has come home to after thirty-one years working construction in California. He is waiting to receive his first Pension Cheque. Twice, in his lifetime, the little home in the bay was destroyed by the ocean. Once in 1946 when he was fifteen and once in 1970 when he was away in California. Now he sleeps in a little trailer and lives outside under a tarp. Maybe he will build a new house next year? His job is to look after the turtles that are plentiful and can be seen from the shore, asses up in the air as they dive. The man and the woman and Koumaka talk. They talk politics; bullshit American politics of greed. They talk about the children playing on boards in the surf. "They don't hurt anyone," Koumaka says. "Ya, just having fun in the ocean," the woman says, as if remembering a childhood freedom. She seems ready to jump off the rock into the ocean, to become one of the turtles.

Koumaka talks about the rice he eats and the fish he catches and how good turtle meat tasted in the old days, when you could still eat them. When it is time to go the woman says, "May I take your picture?" and Koumaka says, "Why?" and the man says to Koumaka, "Because you're so damn good lookin'." They all three laugh. The groom steps back, Koumaka makes his stand and the woman takes the picture.

Afterwards, driving up the hill, the bride says, "I would stay on that black beach with Koumaka, even though he has no teeth." They both laugh and the groom says, "And he would teach you something about loving a man."

That night the man woke from more unwanted dreams. He thought the sea was making a new sound. He got up from his bed, dressed and left the hotel. He walked toward the mournful sound that seemed to be calling a lost lover from across the ocean. The man crouched in the bushes to listen.

Why were they chanting and blowing those big shells across the water? Who was the person with the red halo of curling hair? Short and square, standing in the water, skin glistening white in the moonlight. Man or Woman? It was difficult to tell in that light, from that distance. Anyway, the person with the twisted talking stick raised in the right hand, the single voice calling. And the conch shells, blown by the brown skinned people, responded. And a murmur of deep voices rose and fell with the surf as if there was a chorus of sleepy singers under the water.

And why on this beach in front of the hotel? Why meet here? This is a big island, in some places there are no people. So why here? Pressed face to face with the tourist trade.

The next morning the festival began right beside the hotel. A festival in praise of Lono, the lover-god who would return someday from across the ocean.

And in the crucible days that followed the bride and groom discovered the temple that was hidden on the beach behind the hotel swimming pool, found the Great King's canoe and his talking stick. And hidden beneath the broken down stone wall the carved post to the God Lono.

This was the reason the native priest had said, "This place is special. This place you have chosen to be married." This was the reason the festival was here; to be near the ancient temple and the bones of their kings.

During the festival days the bride and groom went to The Mother Volcano. They stood fearful as mice at these portals, imagining fiery plumes thousands of feet into the air. They threw branches into the pit and shouted from the cliff,

"A place for man to stand."

They followed the road that winds between the caldrons, between the brewing pits for new land, down and down six thousand feet to the ocean where towers of sulphuric steam gush into the air and the hot rock flows unstoppable into the sea and the future is breaking surface.

They danced all night to the festival bands, local island music. The bands played a lazy sort of blues that had forgotten the hard core of its pain in this gentle climate. And they washed away their sweat in the warm ocean, soft as new skin over old bodies.

On the last night of the festival the woman dreamt of azure waters and brightly coloured fishes waving from the rock crevices, calling her down. The deeps were black and bottomless and she was fearless and lithe and naked, swimming deeper and deeper, following the turtles, searching the caverns till dawn. She woke with seaweed in her hair and her skin moist, her muscles swimming smooth. And the man, finally, dreamt of nothing at all.

Now they were both drowning and no longer cared. They saw the world as if from under the water. From this perspective the world was at moments crystal clear and full of magic and, at other moments, their deaths seemed imminent.

The Hand of God

Corporal Jack Melon got the shit shot out of himself in Vietnam. They took him back home to Texas, a vegetable, and put him in a hospital and changed his diaper and rolled him over a couple of times a day to keep him from getting bed sores. There was a part of Jack that knew where he was and understood all too well the predicament he was in. That part could see his body in the hospital bed and roamed the hospital halls and out of the hospital into the world looking for a way to get back to being Jack, the mighty soldier and fornicator. He was looking for a way back to the land of the living but he was trapped in a place that wrapped around the world like a gray cocoon, a muddy mist. Trapped in a half-way world for the dead and the dying. A dark plain just outside the living, where creatures not quite human try desperately to return to their lives on earth.

There are places in that awful land where the membrane that separates the living from the dead is worn thin. The creatures look through the membrane like we look into a pool and they see the land of the living like a mirage in the bottom of the pool. These creatures gather at the pools that bubble across the barren land. They peer into the pools lustfully and stir their fingers in the water; they yearn so badly to return to the earth. Just once more to rip flesh, taste blood. What a horrible sight to see across this desolate plain. For miles and miles they gather in groups according to the terrible sins they have committed. Each tribe more terrible than the last. The creatures act out their crimes again and again. There are no living victims so they use each other in a parody of life. Then, when their fury is spent, they sit quietly and stare in the pools, spying on the living, dreaming of the good old days when they were free to pillage the earth.

Jack moved like a shadow among the groups, peering into pools. He skirted the edges of this lawless society, staying in the darkness. Some crimes he considered too distasteful and beneath his pride. But actually honour had nothing to do with it. Those crimes were not useful to his purpose, so he carried on.

✦ ✦ ✦

A young girl lived in a little town thousands of miles north from the hospital in Texas. Karen was just learning to be a witch and she delighted in the things she could do. She could foretell some events and sometimes she could bend people to her will. Her vision was getting wider and sometimes she could see the raggedy edges of a hole torn in the wall of her father's house. A little hole, behind the sofa, and a wind sucking in and out of that hole as gentle and hot as a sleeping cat's breath. The raggedy edge of the wall rustled like the sound of aspen trees in the breeze, like many small and distant tambourines.

She lived with her father who was fat and drank lots of

beer and didn't ever think about things like holes in the fabric of the world or the strange creatures that lived through those holes. He thought about hockey scores.

In the day, Karen walked in the beautiful park that was in the little town. She met her friends in the park and they sat on the grass and talked about astral travel and the downfall of western civilization. Jimmy worked as a gardener in the park and he joined the conversation, now and again, talking over his shoulder as he weeded the seed beds or planted another 2000 bloody petunias. Petunias were big with the tourists. Jimmy would keep an eye peeled for the foreman, who was always sneaking up on him, then he'd take a quick toke from the joint Karen and her friends were smoking and he'd go back to weeding his flower bed.

Jimmy liked working in the park and he liked listening to the conversations about magic and unseen powers that moved the world and spirits in the forest. He liked to think about Rip Van Winkle drinking the Faerie mead and sleeping for forty years. He liked to think about how small people were and how people never really knew what forces shaped their lives. He didn't like it when Karen talked about Jack, the man with his body in a hospital in Texas.

Karen was friends with Dan, a man from Indiana. Dan thought he was a warlock but he couldn't even jump over a small tree or fart so loud the houses shook. He wore feathers and lit candles. One night Karen and Dan lit their candles and invoked spirits to come forth. Karen wanted to test herself to see what she could bring out. She was a young woman, after all, and, for her, this was seduction. Dan was just chanting to get laid. They were getting rolling, filling the air with incense and incantation, when

one of Karen's friends waltzed in,

"Oh wow," she said passing her hands like a benediction over the candles.

"Look what I got, man," she said to Karen as she settled cross-legged on the floor. She brought out a witch's board. A board with the alphabet on it and a pointer that slides over the board to the letters and spells a message from beyond, if the spirits are willing. One of THOSE boards. They, all three, put their fingers on the pointer.

"Oh wow," said the girl as the pointer began to shake under the weight of their combined fingers. The pointer shook and spun around the board like a drunk driver in a snow storm. The pointer ran off the edge of the board and onto the coffee table. Karen could feel the hair on the back of her neck stand up and her whole body tingle. Dan got a hard on.

Jack was getting desperate. The body in the hospital bed was getting weaker and it was his body. The thread that he crawled back along to get to that body was getting thinner and thinner. He was stretching that thread longer and longer as he wandered over this dismal land, this land of bad odour, of swamps and smoke stacks and horrible creatures that were forever changing shapes. He wandered out with his lifeline, like Hansel and Gretel and their stupid bread crumbs, and he crawled back along that thread like a drunk on his hands and knees trying to find his way home. He crawled back to make sure that sack of flesh he called himself was still breathing. There was no doubt he was dying. He could hear the nurses moving through the room of vegetables where he was kept.

The Hand of God

"This one won't last long," he heard one of the nurses say.

"Hell, sometimes they can hang on like that for years," the other nurse replied.

But Jack knew the first nurse was right. The birds had eaten most of his bread crumbs and soon he wouldn't be able to come back. He would be trapped.

That night, with the help of some friends, permanent boarders in that half-way world for the spirits of the criminally insane; that prison world for diseased souls; that clanging, grinding factory where the chaff of humanity wail incessantly. That night he was brought to the pool by the child killers and he could see Karen and Dan and The Girl at the bottom of the murky pool. The child killers showed Jack how he could dip his fingers into the pool and stir up the people on the other side. They taught him how to attract the weak ones.

Jack discovered he could talk to Karen and Dan and The Girl. The three of them sat in the basement room. The candles fluttered and, upstairs, the wind sucked through the hole in the wall behind the couch and Karen's father snoozed in his favourite chair.

The pointer spun beneath their fingers. Jack, like dipping a stick in the water of the pool, stirred his thoughts across the board, letter by letter. He was so excited at first, the pointer was bouncing off the walls. When he finally settled down he spelled out who he was.

"My name is Jack," he began, and over the next few nights the story of his imprisonment in a vegetable body in Texas and his travels through this weird half-way world were told by the spinning, halting pointer.

✦ ✦ ✦

"The tests are positive," Jimmy heard The Girl say to Karen as the two girls sat on the grass in the park. The Girl was pregnant. She had missed two periods. "What am I going to do?" she said, "My dad will kill me and I'll have to drop out of college." She was a picture of dejection. Karen said, "Let's see what the witch's board says, maybe it can give us an answer."

✦ ✦ ✦

Jack could almost touch the girl. He could feel life growing in her belly. He placed his hand on top of the pool and felt the pulse of innocent, unborn life rise like a small bubble to the surface. He promised the child killers anything if they would bring him to this pool again. If they would help him take what he needed and go back to his body in Texas. He spoke to the creatures as if they were soldiers. He said, "I will find real victims, small bundles of flesh and blood, and bring them close to you and you can watch me kill them." They nodded. They laughed. They wanted Jack to live. He would be their tongue, to taste life. He would bring them sustenance. He would touch the things they were not allowed to touch. He would bring them fresh blood. They were happy to be of service. They brought Jack to the pool again and again. Sometimes Jack sat quietly watching Dan and The Girl and Karen. And sometimes he stirred them up. Touched them and made them shiver.

✦ ✦ ✦

Karen loved to have Jack at her beck and call. It made her feel powerful and sexy. She screwed Dan thinking about Jack, the great fighter and fornicator. She could feel Jack's presence hovering over Dan when they made love. She could feel Jack's hands touching her. Dan was a real stud that first night. He came three times and licked Karen's pussy until she was crazy. He put his fingers inside her, and his cock at the same time, and sucked on her tits, and Jack from through the hole laughed to see what comical lust he could inspire with a little help from his friends, the child killers.

Jack could feel the little baby in The Girl's belly. The baby was an old spirit coming back to earth after a rest in the water-washed sunlight of earned oblivion. She had her destiny to fulfill, no more sleeping through the ages, it was time to be born. She had shaken herself free from freedom and plummeted down into the girl's womb. Her hopeful path was laid out in intricate possibilities before her. She was ready to begin again.

Jack needed the baby. Karen and Dan would help him. They loved him. He made their candles flutter. Jack invented amazing prophecies for the future to impress them. He wrote sad poetry on the witch's board and then he wrote, "I will take the baby back." As if he were doing them all a big favour.

✦ ✦ ✦

The Girl thought God Himself had spoken. Jack could feel an opening between the wings of the Angels that protect little babies. The wings of the Angels are motivated by the love of a mother. They beat faster when there is more love. The Angel's wings were heavy, laden down with confusion from The Girl's mind. The Girl thought God wanted her baby back. She had heard Him speak. The Angels thought they were in the wrong place.

✦ ✦ ✦

Jimmy was working in the park, weeding a rampant bed, and Karen came up to him and asked him what he thought about Jack taking the baby? Once she started talking she couldn't stop. She said,

"Jack wants to take the baby and The Girl thinks Jack is God, speaking through the witch's board. She doesn't want the baby anyway."

"The whole thing stinks," Jimmy said, massaging the back of his neck. He didn't like thinking about that little baby and this guy, Jack, eating the baby's soul, and the fetus in a garbage can somewhere. He didn't like thinking, but he couldn't help himself. His mind went around and around the horrible pictures.

Dan came up and said,

"The baby's going to die anyways, so what's the difference? If Jack can use it, why not?"

"The whole business makes me sick," Jimmy said, "What are you getting out of this, Dan? And you, Karen?" Karen would not look up from her shoes but the colour rose in her cheeks. Dan stood very straight and defiant, cocksure. Jimmy shook his head and carried on with his chores. The fat, sweating, pig of a foreman was trying to sneak up on him again. He could see him across the field peering through his coke bottle glasses from behind a big tree. Usually this would have made Jimmy happy. Jimmy would keep retreating just outside the foreman's sight. The foreman would sneak from tree to tree, peering down the tunnels of his vision searching to catch Jimmy loafing, his face getting redder and redder, stinking sweat in big round stains flowing from his armpits and down his back, the veins on his temples ready to burst. He would grunt across the lawns from tree to tree, blind and angry. But today there was no joy in the chase and Jimmy stayed where he was and weeded the garden.

"I don't know much about The Girl," Jimmy said, "and I don't know anything about the baby. But everyone deserves a chance, Dan, even you." And he weeded with a heavy heart.

Karen barely listened to Jimmy. She was so infatuated with all the excitement she was in the middle of. Besides, she had never been fucked like this before and she wanted to help her lover, Jack, get back to his living self. Perhaps she had the romantic notion that he would find her, here in this little town. He would arrive in living flesh, driving a brand new Buick with Texas plates. Reborn.

And Dan? He never was much of a lover before Jack came along and now he was heroic. Confident as a killer stalking his prey. He knew the perfect touch. When to linger and when to strike. Oh yes, he loved Jack.

◆ ◆ ◆

Jack was getting impatient. He couldn't reach through and grab the baby. He didn't have the power and neither did his evil friends. They weren't allowed to steal babies. They lived forever with their desire for carnage unfulfilled.

The creatures rolled over each other and bit each other and fought to look through the hole into the world of real flesh and blood where Karen and Dan and The Girl were coming closer and closer. They hunched down by the hole to wait.

"Just like fishing through the ice," Jack thought. He dropped a line into the pool. The line descended like a thin dark snake through the murky water. The creatures were quiet, still, tense. Below, in the basement room, Karen held The Girls head and stroked her hair. Dan pulled her skirt up and pushed her legs apart.

The Girl held herself open and the line floated down and slipped inside her and wound tightly in coils around the baby's soul. Seven deadly coils. Dan chanted. The candles fluttered.

From the other side, Jack pulled the line and there was a little wet "plop" and a small blue flash across the room. A flash you weren't even certain you'd seen. Maybe there was a small moan like a child going back to sleep. The baby's soul was gone. Within hours The Girl aborted the fetus. Dan flushed it down the toilet.

In the moment when Jack ate the little soul, he felt nothing. Almost like gulping air. He looked at the creatures and the creatures looked at him. Quizzical.

Then the thin loose thread that stretched out between the boiling pits, the bird-eaten thread that held Jack to his body in Texas, began to move, to swell and pulse with blood. The line became elastic with life, tightened, and yanked Jack head over heels across the gray land. He was pulled thousands of miles across the plain in a flash, whipped down the hospital halls in a blur and snapped roughly back into his body. He sat straight up in his hospital bed howling and laughing. The nurses came running and shot him full of morphine.

"A miraculous recovery," the nurses said.
"The hand of God," Jack's mother said.

Heartbreak Hotel

In those days I was living in the house the Englishman had built on the cliff above the water. I could watch the weather blow up and down the lake through the big picture window. Behind the house an old orchard grew. The apple trees still flourished, despite years of neglect, fed by an underground spring.

There were apples in that orchard no longer grown; Cox's Orange, Gravenstein, Winter Banana, Tumbler's Ecstasy, and a large, misshapen, discoloured and unnamed apple that was the sweetest and juiciest of all. Apples planted at the turn of the century by the opium smoking Englishman, picked up in the autumn by the paddlewheel steamer and shipped back down the lake to the village where, had we been born a half century sooner, we would have stood, all knickers and licorice, and watched the apples steam in.

In summer I worked thirty miles away in town as a gardener. Every morning as the sun was rising I would drive along the winding lake road. I rarely met another car until I had passed through the Indian Reservation and was going around the head of the lake. In winter I stayed close to home with my dog, my goats and my chickens for company.

About the time I was settling in for winter, Kye and Allison and Allison's daughter Kitty were leaving San Francisco. They packed their stuff into a blue Volkswagen and headed north, running to Canada. By early spring they were setting up home in an abandoned log house, two miles up the mountain behind my place.

The first shocked nights in the old house were loud with silence. The wind blew down the mountain and through the fir trees. The trees creaked in the wind. Branches rubbed together. The silence was deafening after the raucous nights at concerts, at parties in crowded rooms, at love-ins in the park. People in motion on the streets. San Francisco had been wild and loud. Now, every sound sneaked away like a fugitive, was absorbed into the forest.

They renovated the log house that sat in the high meadow. They had a beautiful view for miles north and south up and down the lake. And eastward the hills receded into layer after layer of deepening blue. They could see all the way to the snow-capped Monashee Mountains.

Kye worked hard. He shovelled cow dung off the floors and washed them on his hands and knees. He chinked between the logs, mixing mud and straw in a bucket. He fixed the doors and windows. He chopped firewood and he painted numerous, surreal pictures of Allison against a hot-blue Okanagan sky. Soon, the old log house in the meadow was transformed.

Antiques arrived. A big old pump organ was installed in the living room. Persian rugs for the floors. Armchairs and sofas. Upstairs, a four-poster bed with a canopy.

Allison wore satins and silks, velour and lace. Or she wore nothing at all and lay about on cushions.

But there was something hanging around that place. One day I was walking in the lower meadow and when the house was out of sight, I couldn't get back. The air behind me was too thick to walk through. I kept walking but I was getting scared. I could hear horses pounding through the pine forest on both sides of the meadow, the riders shouting and cracking their whips against the trees. I thought they were the Scottish ancestors who once owned this land and they were going to get me. Every step the air became thicker. I turned and ran back. I was running in a dream and getting nowhere. My limbs were sleepy and every movement was an effort. I was sweating and my heart was thumping against my ribs. Finally, I burst free from the confines of this apparition, waking with a start, and scrambled up the slope to the house. I sat panting and shivering on the verandah and the grasshoppers resumed their lazy summer melody.

Another time I was sitting in my old truck outside the house. The damn truck wouldn't start; maybe she was flooded, so I was waiting to try again. My little black dog was sitting beside me. The moon was rising over the tin roof. The moon seemed to get younger as I sat there. The house seemed newer. I heard a child's voice, sad and very far away. Then closer, louder, and sadder. My little dog growled and jumped, snarling at the window, though there was nothing to be seen.

Ghosts were hanging around that house. They got Allison. The wild riders in the pine forest, the sad moon-child from long ago and that old Scotswoman, last of the settlers, alone in that big stone mansion down on the lakeshore, waiting to die. They were all whispering in Allison's ears, spinning her round and round.

The house in the high meadow had been part of a larger estate. The dying Scotswoman was the last of a wealthy family who had settled this remote land. For years there had been no road, only the paddlewheel steamer to bring supplies and take away the apples. Now she hobbled around inside her huge stone house down on that isolated shore. She never went outside. At night, there were no lights shining through the windows.

Allison went down and had tea with the Scotswoman. They talked about the weather but a deeper current ran through their meeting. They met several times in the darkened house and Allison brought the old lady soup. Allison could hear the woman's voice inside her head. After each visit the voice was louder and clearer.

A few months later the woman lay dying in the stone house and Allison sat upstairs in the house in the high meadow. They communicated across the distance, met on another plane. Allison said,

"When the old woman died we had tea together, after the funeral, chatting in our ethereal bodies."

Allison began walking like that scrawny old woman, shuffling around and pointing her finger when she talked. Her voice became sharp and high, wavering demands imperiously over the lowered heads of Kye and Kitty.

When winter began, Allison wouldn't come outside. She stayed by the woodstoves. Kye chopped wood, cooked and kept the stoves burning cherry red. He painted pictures of Allison reclining warmly on red cushions, snow-laden fir trees dancing outside her window. The silent Okanagan sky, cool and distant.

One day I went up to the house and Allison said, "Did you notice something special about yesterday?" and I said, "Yes, it was a nice day, with rosy clouds like twilight, all day long, very pretty." And she said, "Is that all?" and I said, "Yes," and she said, "I thought you were more in tune than that, 'cause yesterday we stopped the world for a couple of minutes."

Allison was constantly moving her furniture around. She moved it carefully. She believed her possessions to be a microcosm for the whole world. She believed by dragging a sofa across the living room floor she could balance the world like a ball on a seal's nose, and slip us all into timelessness. Only for a moment. Only the most sensitive beings would feel the shift from time to timelessness and back again. I was not among them.

Early in the winter Kye came down to my place. He said a gang had taken over his house; just moved right in. "They came out of nowhere," he said.

The gang of seven had been there a couple of days, he said. He wanted me to help him. We got into my old truck and drove up to the house in the meadow.

Two strong guys, naked to the waist, were outside chopping and piling wood in the frosty air. Inside, five pimply-faced boys did housework or lay about on the sofas. The antique sofas so carefully, so cosmically, positioned by Allison. Allison and Kitty had run away. They were staying with American friends in a mansion south of town, miles away.

The two strong guys stopped chopping and came inside and we all stood in the kitchen. They crossed their arms and looked us over. We asked them to pack up and get out. I said, "This house belongs to Kye and Allison and you should leave." They said, "Allison invited us by letter, to join her commune." They had come all the way from Montreal and they were going to stay. They said, "Everyone can stay, one big happy family, no problem," and they smiled. Kye said "No way, you have to leave," and the two guys both grabbed knives off the counter and chased us outside.

We sped off down the mountain, white faces, white knuckles, and left them to perform Satanic rituals in the four-poster bed, to defile the Persian rugs. Kye called the cops and the cops kicked them out but I kept a gun under my bed for a couple of months after that. Living alone, so far away from people, I was afraid they would slice me open in the middle of the night.

Allison made it through most of the winter without incident, but in March she dragged all her clothes and furniture outside the house. She put them in a pile and burned them. I had walked up through the forest on the corn snow; the road was not plowed. I watched her from behind the trees. She was shuffling around the fire like an old woman, poking a stick at the pile of burning stuff. Acrid black smoke was billowing up into a cool blue sky. The yard was littered with things she was bringing to the fire. Chairs and pictures and trunks full of clothes. A treadle sewing machine. She was talking to herself, arguing loudly in a Scottish accent. There was no one else around.

I came out from my hiding place in the trees. As soon as she saw me she changed. "I'm having a party," she waved and shouted. She didn't look old anymore and the Scottish accent was gone. She moved smoothly. She danced a little. She flirted with me and showed me her tits. I stood beside her, looking into the fire. I said, "Nice party, Allison." Then she said, "Let's go to your place and have a party." But I said, "No way," and shook my head. Allison got mad. She danced around the fire in her flowing clothes, waving her arms in front of her face. She put the evil eye on me. So I left.

I could hear her yelling as I made my way between the pine trees on the crusty snow. Her curses were a dark counterpoint to the warm spring wind, the sparkling blue sky, and the intermittent voices of the chickadees and crows.

A couple of days later a friend was visiting me from town. She was doing the breakfast dishes and looking out the window up the dirt track that led to my house on the cliff. The days had been warm, thawing the snow, but the nights were cold and there was jagged ice on the roads. She said, "Kye is coming down the road." She paused, "He's playing his guitar." I glanced up and grunted from my book and porridge. "And," she said, "He's not wearing any clothes." She wiped the plate clean and raised her eyebrows ever so slightly.

"Take some clothes," I said to him. "Stand by the fire. Have a cup of tea." He refused all three and stood at the doorway shrivelling. Finally, he did take a blanket and wrapped it around himself to get warm, but also out of shyness for that pitiful little blue thing, peeking sadly from between his legs. "Allison sent me to tell you the world is going to end," Kye said. He kept his head down and spoke to the ground. His straight dark hair falling around his pale face. "I know that," I said. "You do?" he replied.

Then, satisfied that his mission was accomplished, he left my house, shedding the blanket but accepting a pair of wool socks to protect his bleeding feet. We watched the cheeks of his frozen white arse fighting each other up the hill until they disappeared.

Shortly after that Allison and Kye carried little Kitty, upside down, naked and screaming, all the way down the mountain road to the lake road. Almost two miles. Allison walked behind, shouting encouragement. She said the demons were pouring out the top of Kitty's head and going back into the earth. Kye did the dirty work, holding Kitty by her ankles. Kye felt bad the next day and he came to my house and asked me to take Kitty for a while.

So Kitty came to stay with me, in the house on the cliff. Kitty and I ate porridge together in the morning and looked out the big picture window over the lake. We made toast on top of the woodstove. The entire house smelled sweetly burnt. We ate the homemade bread that tasted like nuts and we ate our porridge covered in fresh cream so thick it had to be spooned from the jar. And brown sugar, of course, and cups of herbal tea.

The turbulence of the weather seemed to flow around our little house and log barn perched on the cliff over the lake. Sometimes I could feel a cold wind slipping through the orchard when I was pruning trees, but the house and the tiny log barn felt quiet and safe. The gusting winds could not break into our haven.

I did see Allison one night, standing like a ghost beside my bed. She was draped seductively in a diaphanous gown and she touched her breasts and her soft, blonde pubic hair. She beckoned me to touch her but I refused, feeling a malevolence, a deceit, a malignance, and she faded into the dawn.

Once a week, during the winter, I walked down the road to get milk from the farmer who lived two miles to the north. He had a jersey cow that gave twenty-five percent cream and that's why Kitty liked the porridge so much. I visited with the farmer and his wife and he said, "Allison has gone into town. I gave her a ride this morning."

His wife put coffee and fresh buns and homemade butter on the table and said, "I tried to give her some clothes but she wouldn't take them." She was a kindly woman and her voice was full of concern.

Allison had hitched a ride into town with the farmer. She stepped out from behind a fir tree wearing a fur coat and slippers, nothing else. She said she was going to a party and asked the farmer to take her to the police station 30 miles away in town. So he did.

Allison convinced the police to drive her south of town to visit her friends. The friends, Scott and Jill, were fellow expatriate Americans who lived in a mansion belonging to Jill's father. The mansion was on a park-like peninsula that jutted out into a turquoise lake. Allison told the cop she was going to a skating party. The cop said, "There's no ice on the lake, it's all melted." Allison said, "There will be when I get there."

When Scott and Jill looked out the windows of their mansion, they saw huge fir trees and the mingling branches of a cherry orchard. The orchard ran right down to the sand at the water's edge. Reeds and bulrushes scrubbed the lapping water. Lily pads floated in the little bay.

When the cop car pulled up the long drive, the sound of toilets flushing disturbed the bucolic serendipity of this small world. Scott and Jill went running through the house digging out the stashes and disposing of their precious contraband. They peered through the drapes, conjectures racing through their minds.

Allison emerged from the cop car like visiting royalty. She no longer moved like an old woman. She was playing the tart now. She kissed both cops on the cheek and let her coat fall open. The cops reddened. "She's all yours, buddy," the cop said to Scott, and they took off.

Allison waved goodbye as the cop car sped down the drive. She turned to Scott, standing weakly on the stairs. She said, "I have arrived for the party" and she flounced inside and took her fur coat off. She danced naked. She ripped the drapes from the huge lead-glass windows and wrapped them around herself. She tried to start a fire on the hardwood floor, using her fur coat and the curtains as fuel. Scott grabbed her and threw her outside. Her eyes narrowed and her lips pulled back in a snarl. After that she was gone, I don't know where.

A few months later, when the apple trees were in bloom, Allison and Kye came to get Kitty. They drove down the steep driveway and parked on the edge of the cliff. We had tea. Kitty didn't want to go and I should have kept her, but I didn't. She gave me a piercing look that disturbs me to this day. As if I were a judge and had pronounced sentence on her. And maybe I had. I watched them load her into the blue Volkswagen beetle. They drove up to the house in the high meadow where Kye had painted, during Allison's absence, in red script on the tin roof, "HEART-BREAK HOTEL". The house was empty now, cleared out, the furniture shipped. They drove down the mountain road and then north around the head of the lake. I never saw them again.

The Birth of Faust
for Sveva Caetani

As I lay curled on my couch upon an afternoon, with the long meadow stretching outside my tall windows, I dreamt the falling of sleepy souls from long travel into my valley. "They are mulch for my garden," I heard someone say and looking up I saw the souls floating down like notes through the crystal air. They fell from a great height and laced the sky with silver tracers. They sunk with a sigh into the soft loam.

   I slept downstairs in the Victorian mansion and upstairs the children, grown outside in the garden of souls, invented plays to bring downstairs in the evening. Through the evening they danced the centuries in intricate detail; their costumes changing seamlessly as the years unfolded. And on and on I dreamt through the centuries as the clouds scudded by outside and souls fell from the clouds like rain. And they fell from the clouds like snow. And they fell like sleet driving against the tall panes of glass.

   And still I slept and the children danced upon my eyelids through the summers and winters, danced crazy quilts patchwork, danced cathedral colours till dawn, danced loss, pain and deep purple dusk, until I was blind and bleeding and stumbled from my mansion and stumbled out of my valley and awoke myself to this lonely stretch of road.

So you find me here. I am ready to be born and already old. Already the palsied shake. The eyeballs all white and roadmap. My eyelids are torn to shreds by those beautiful tiny feet, my retina shattered by the lyrical intensity of their voices. I have no other memory. Memories are like dreams before other dreams; they are gone with the waking and leave only a feeling, an aftertaste, a discontent.

Those mischievous children have bewitched me. Down I fell upon the couch and could not turn my eyes from their mesmeric dance, their plays. My eyes are burned with their light. I am blinded.

Along this cold, dark road I ply my careful way, lit only by the wavering candle of my inner sight. Ha, I see from out these useless orbs, these eyes gone mad! I see the sense of things, if not the things themselves. My inner sight is a tapping white cane through the towering trees; a stuttering shuffle toward the lights in the distance.

With each step I feel flesh forming like a cocoon around me. The weavers, they drive their needles through the thin line of charged light that is me. They tie my little flame, through a million spear points, to this wanting flesh. They follow me, hooded and dark, through the forest alongside the road. The only light that escapes their dense, dark, magnetism are the needles they throw flashing across the road, piercing my thin flame.

And I hear wings flapping through the crow forest: fluttering around a birth. I see my own birth in the village below me as I stand at the edge of this great forest and look down at the small cluster of lights.

They will make man of me, these weavers, these needles, these binding threads. The weavers tie flesh to bone and bone to fire. The little flame struggles continually to be free from the thousands of punctures and the tight lace, the corset of flesh. But the new threads are strong and the wounded flame is weak.

Down I go, flying and falling, into the metropolis. Not even my mother will see these scarred, old eyes hidden behind such pretty new flesh.

Behind the Fence

We knew nothing of royalty in our little town, so far away from the big events of the world. We had the Coldstream-English with their pretensions to aristocracy, gentility and the graces of culture, but their secrets were dusty and dull.

There was one Countess, though. One magnificent, long limbed, dark eyed, mysterious Countess, striding out with her basket (covered with a white linen cloth) down Pleasant Valley Road. Striding out darkly and quickly with her little handmaiden right behind, three short maid steps to one long royal step. Long dark skirts rustling, shawls covering, pale skin glowing, beneath the big fir trees, along the dirt path.

Our Countess lived with her mother and an old family servant, little Miss Juule, in the white mansion on Pleasant Valley Road. The mansion was surrounded by thick forest and a high wooden fence. And behind the fence big, white, wild dogs roamed the woods. The gate was always shut and if you walked too near the fence you could hear the dogs pawing and snuffling at the earth to get at your tender flesh.

In the winter we children ride our sleds down the field beside the fence. Behind the fence there is an unholy silence undisturbed by our laughing and shouting as we haul our sleds up the slope. We slide and climb and sneak into the barn at the top of the slope and smell the musk of hay and wood and horseshit. From the loft of the barn we can see over the fence.

The mystery is there, upstairs in the big house, where the mother stands with her back to the heat register, fingers entwined in the warm metal coils. She is cold. She is always cold. Mother lives upstairs and never goes outside and nobody ever sees her. The rumours of her madness are whispered over our small heads at five o'clock suppers, whispered between neighbours over backyard fences. The endless rumours. We climb into the barn's loft. We think we see a shadow moving across an upstairs window.

In those days there were mostly woodlands along Pleasant Valley Road. That was the place we had our forts and secret trails. Once in a while the big gates opened, just a crack, and out slipped the great Countess Caetani and right behind her the bird-like Miss Juule. The Royal Progression had begun! All down the street the message was relayed by little couriers, breathless from the race down wooded trails and potholed alleys and over backyard fences,

"The countess is coming, the countess is coming," they cried, and we sneaked and hid and followed behind and raced ahead to watch The Royal Shopping.

Quickly down Pleasant Valley Road and down Lovers' Lane and down the hill past the granite court house, built by Italian craftsman. Quickly over the tracks and past the red brick station. Quickly down Main Street they go, filling their baskets. And we are belly and backside to dirty brick and block, hiding between two buildings on Main Street, waiting for the Countess to pass. Each store they enter we note, remark upon, discuss in whispers from behind the trunks of the huge maple trees that line both sides of the street and form a green canopy overhead. The trees wave their leafy heads above us and mute the light all down the street in tones of filtered green.

In this verdant light she buys her thread and needles at Stedman's Five and Ten Cent Store. Across the street and half a block down she buys her cloth at The Fabric Shop, chatting briefly with the plump woman behind the counter. She stops at The White Heather Bakery to buy bread and a sweet roll from the frugally-built Scottish woman. Eyes straight ahead she strides past The Spudnut Shop where the ex-navy man, tattooed up the hairy arms and smelling of the world, dips potato dough in hot grease to make the light and fluffy pastry. No stopping here.

Last stop is The Maple Leaf Grocery where she makes her order, watched intently from the backroom by the delivery boy, eyes wide through the crack in the rough wooden wall, ears absorbing the sound of patent leather shoes on the plank floor. She uses the phone in the back of the store to call Mother. She says, "Right away Mama, we are almost home." And now they must hurry, little Miss Juule and The Countess, quickly across the tracks and up the hill. A polite and regal nod, a short exchange of pleasantries to any passerby. But quickly the gate swings shut, and locks them up tight again, to Mother.

And we are hid, breathless, in the bushes across the road, watching them disappear. At night, we lie in bed and think about the mother, upstairs, washing her money. And we think about the long, pale face of our Countess, absorbing the silence, as if she belongs to the moon.

✦ ✦ ✦

One night of the year the gate swung open and stayed open. The dogs were confined to their kennels. The children, dressed as spirits of the dead and carrying pillow cases for their treats, wandered cautiously, clinging together in groups, up the long, shaded drive.

So late in the year, so late in the night, for little children, dressed so bravely in their costumes, to be out and alone on the dark forest street. The big cottonwood trees waved in the frosty wind and dry leaves crackled underfoot. The gate was open like a mouth and the long dark drive was the throat, descending into the belly of madness. Yet, at the end of the drive was a succulent promise of the very best treats in town! Every goblin and pirate and fairy and ghost and princess and cat and cowboy and clown was rushing to the open gates.

Only once did I muster courage and run the gauntlet of dark trees and dense underbrush, up the long drive, to reach the small circle of golden light. I pounded on the dutch-door and held my pillow sack up, hoping for the orange and black box, shaped like a lantern, hung from a string, that I had seen the others gaily swinging. A black and orange box that looked as though the moon were shining from inside, to silhouette the black cats prancing and arching their backs. You could see the black, electrified hair standing on end and the lips curled back to show sharp teeth. And inside? Foreign chocolates with soft centres!

The top-half of the door opened and I said, "Trick or treat," knowing there would be no tricks at this door. And a stern voice in a thick accent said, "There is no more. You are too late. You must go away." The door closed and the witches were done with giving out favours. They had darker rituals to attend. The dogs were whining to be set free.

Now I must run the dark driveway without the warm protection of that candied lamp to drive away the shadows. The dogs will rip me to pieces. I have been found unworthy to carry a lamp and must be killed. Why me?

Because Mother stands facing the wall in her upstairs room and she can see me, with that other sight, as plain as the nose on your face. Her eye is everywhere on this property. She can see my bad thoughts. She can see me, even beyond the fence, in my bed at night, curled around my painful belly, frightened and ashamed.

Mother has an eye to root out sin. She sees in every nook and cranny where the young Countess might hide a girlish thought. A poem for love. A thought scribbled on a scrap of paper and hidden in our Countess's frock, is discovered, is a transgression! A priest is called in, so our Countess can confess this sin of vanity. A soft dab of paint on paper is burned to crisp under Mother's eye.

"Wasting time with your paints, girl, wasting time with your foolish thoughts." Girl! She was hardly a girl anymore. The years went by. The gate stayed shut and our Countess was locked up tight.

✦ ✦ ✦

Duke Leone Caetani di Sermoneta arrived in our little town from Rome via London in 1921. He inquired at his club in London where a gentleman might travel to put down new roots. The time had come to leave Italy behind. Centuries of tyrannical rule by the church and now the fascists. He would be singled out. His liberal ideas had alienated him from his powerful and conservative family and class. And the fascists would kill him. These are the reasons he gave for leaving.

But he had other reasons not spoken. So Leone, the 15th Duke of Sermoneta, at the age of 54, came west to escape the confinement of his birth. He left behind a career in the Italian parliament, respect, power, a marriage gone cold and the disappointment of a retarded son. He brought with him his new wife, beautiful Ofelia, 30 years younger than himself. And their little girl, our Countess. And the young wife and the child of sin; they were the reason for leaving.

The Englishmen at his club in London said, "Everyone is going to the Okanagan Valley in Canada to grow apples and swim in the lakes. It's marvelous." Leone had been here before, in his youth. He had shot a bear and he remembered the wildness. So the three exiles came to our Valley.

Our Countess often told the story of their royal arrival in our little town. A story she probably did not remember, since she was only four at the time, but had been told again and again until it had become her own memory.

How they arrived by train and were met by Mr. Harwood with his team of horses to carry all the baggage. How the men at the station had never seen such a sight and marveled as they unloaded wardrobes full of Mama's clothes. Each wardrobe containing perfect dresses and all the accessories in drawers, one drawer to match each outfit. How they sweated under trunks full of household goods and tools and books. So many books. How she, our little Countess, was all ringlets and ribbons and bows. And Mama. Beautiful Ofelia. Young Ofelia, delicate and pale and dressed in the latest Parisian couture. Mama, the dark beauty of a silent screen movie star, a breathless twenty-three years old, stepping off the train, placing her tiny foot on the platform and taking the hand of her gallant Duke, relying on his tall strength.

Our Countess told me how they travelled about town with the real estate agent and Mother said, "*Non, Non, Non*" to every place until finally, "*si, si, si,*" to the big white house on Pleasant Valley Road.

Leone Caetani embraced the Okanagan: the distance, the freedom. And the dark regrets he harboured were blown away with the constantly changing weather. He swam in the lakes, leaving the shore way behind, until he was a speck in the water between the vacant range hills. Mother sat on the beach under her parasol.

Once, and only once, Leone took Ofelia to the farm where he was cutting down trees. He wanted to show her how he had become a rugged man. A Canadian. Leone set Ofelia on a fallen tree to watch this marvel of science and strength. He chopped at the tree with much flourish and sweat and the tree twisted and fell wrong and landed across the tree where Mama was seated and catapulted poor Mama into the air. Up she went and down she came. She wasn't hurt but she wasn't pleased. That was Ofelia's only visit to the farm. Our Countess remembered this event with a certain joy, like a giggle hidden behind her hand.

For Leone, this little town, these backwards people, were a new challenge. He continued his studies on Islam and published articles in erudite periodicals from far away places. He wrote letters to the Italian newspapers that were not printed. During the days, he explored our country and studied the inhabitants with the sensibilities of a humanist and the acuity of an anthropologist. He was gracious and interested, reaching his hand out and looking a man in the eye. If necessary, he was willing to wade in up to the boot tops.

In his loneliness, the Duke sawed and split and stacked cords and cords of wood. There is a picture of him, somewhere in the archives, one leg up on the chopping block, axe resting across his knee, the piles of wood stretching out behind him into infinity along the fence.

The days slipped by in this new country and only late at night, alone in his study, was he filled with remorse for all the things lost and left behind. The lost things would rise up through him, fill him, burst in his chest, and, still rising, escape as tears and a strangle of sobs. All things lost! And upstairs young Ofelia sleeping, her love cooling, ashes sifting down.

Ofelia never really left Rome. She never learned English. She was embarrassed to make a mistake and too proud to ask, and she was frightened by this big, new country. She did not like the language. English had no passion and pretentious Englishmen were everywhere, strutting about as if they were nobility. Imposters. The only other Italians were ignorant peasants, and far beneath her.

During a rare visit home, to Italy, Ofelia described the

anguished sound of trains running lonely and forever through the night hills of Canada. "Hooww, hoooww," she moaned and put her head back and cried to mimic the train's whistle. This was the sound of her new life, the terrible loss and loneliness she suffered, way out here at the ends of the earth. She had given up everything to follow her Duke, but what choice did she have? She had wanted him so badly; this much older man, this married man and she had pursued him shamelessly. She had caused a scandal through all of Rome, this pale-skinned and dark-haired debutante. She had captured a wild, restless creature. A thirsty man. A lean, hungry man. And, like a wolf, he had picked her up, gently in his mouth, and carried her into this dark, heathen forest. Gone were the great entertainments of Rome's society. The two hundred dresses and two hundred pairs of shoes lay useless. She was cast out.

Leone lived fourteen years in this new country. He died in 1935, when our Countess was seventeen and Mama was only thirty-eight. When Papa died Mama closed the gates and never again left the house. There were no more trips for our young Countess. No more journeys by train and boat and car back to the Villa Miraggio on the top of seventh hill in the centre of Rome. The Villa on fire with a different and glorious view of the city from each window. Each morning, still in nightclothes, running from room to room, a full circle visual feast! Never again.

Our Countess would say, "Mother, Mother, we could start a little shop. Your designs are magnificent. You are brilliant with the cut and the cloth. And I am such a nimble, such an artful, seamstress. We could make a team to rival the great houses of Europe." Or just, "Mother, we could drive into the country and have a picnic overlooking the lake." But the gate stayed shut.

Mother commanded our Countess, and the Chinaman houseboy, to drag the big trunks from the basement. She said, "What I want is in this trunk. The blue trunk. With the emblem. That is the one." And the houseboy said, "Yes Missy," and they brought up the blue trunk and mother opened it and breathed in Rome, Ancient Rome, her youth, her blood, in the smells from that trunk. Then she said, "No, No, this is not the trunk. You must bring the wardrobe, with the lace dresses I wore, so long ago in Cuba, when we travelled and danced." And our Countess and the houseboy hauled the wardrobe up the steep basement stair and up the big main stair to the attic room where mother lived, and mother breathed in Rome.

Our Countess was not really a Countess at all. She was the daughter of a duke so she was a duchess, I suppose. But in our ignorance, the entire town called her "The Countess" and the title stuck. Our Countess said to me,

"Where we come from, counts and countesses are card sharks and pimps. There was a countess in Rome and she insisted on leaving the lights on, inside her limousine, so people could see her riding about in her furs and finery. She would ride around with the lights on, smoking a cigarette in a long gold holder. A bloated caricature of a woman. Can you imagine?" She said this to me, in the last years, when she was laid out in bed and almost completely paralysed. She seemed to fill up the room with those long limbs reaching into every corner. Once again, she had become a prisoner in that house.

She said over and over again during those last haunted nights, "Why Oh Why Oh Why did you do it? Why did you keep me prisoner?"

Even during the day, when we talked, the mention of her mother made her body twist and she pushed her head hard against the pillow, looking away into a darkness beyond me.

"Why did you keep me a prisoner?" she would say, propped against the pillows to breathe. "I would never leave you. You were my mother. I was a loyal daughter. Why oh Why oh why, did you?" And I knew, when no one was there, she rocked herself and cried softly.

✦ ✦ ✦

"For the first 15 years I had the yard to roam but for the last ten years I was kept closely to the house. For entire years I felt I could not breathe. I strangled in my own silent scream. Mother was certain I would abandon her here, exiled in this godforsaken country, where she didn't speak the language. The stress of my willful behaviour would explode her weak heart. She would sit, exhausted and clammy, her heart palpitating, while poor Miss Juule rushed about with cold compresses and hot teas. "My daughter is killing me," she would wail and I would not go where I was going or do what I was doing. I would stay.

"I was allowed to read. Nothing else. No painting, which I yearned for. No writing, which I could not resist, and did secretly, and was punished for again and again. The merciless eye was on me. And read, I did. I ordered books from my catalogue and they came in a big crate, delivered to the door, and I devoured them. I drank them down into my belly. I soared beyond the fence with the masters. The masters were my friends and my lovers. I knew them casually and intimately. My lovers! My friends . . .

"Oh, and the conversations we had, those writers and I! And I had my favourites, dreaming all alone year after year. Rilke, Dante, Madame Murasaki, Shelley, George Sand. I knew every cadence of their works, and we would walk and laugh and drink wine, secretly, in the garden. They were my only joy! My only friends.

"But mother had a second sight and she could see my dreams. She stared at her wall, and saw me dancing in the garden with a handsome man. And kissing him. She saw me talking in the garden with a beautiful woman. And she saw me, beneath the arbour, kissing a woman dressed in a man's suit. Damn her malicious sight! She has stared, day after day, at her damn wall and she has seen into my only secret place. She has seen my vanity, my sensual dreams."

◆ ◆ ◆

Mother, Ofelia, in her attic room year after year. Her life shattered. Only the priest to see her. Not the doctor, he must make his examination from behind the door. Mother speaks to daughter and daughter translates the pains to the doctor. But the doctor must not see her, certainly must not touch her. Only the priest can see her. She washes the money and gives it to the priest. The priest takes the money and pretends not to see the sin of witchcraft added to Ofelia's youthful fornication. Ofelia uses her vision to root out sin in the name of the church and that is justification enough for the priest. He turns his back on the daughter, the prisoner, standing timidly in the hall. Her bowed head seems to accentuate her lanky frame. Her hands are clasped submissively in front of her but she is determined to die. She confesses to the priest her desire to die; she can no longer stand this prison. How many years must she suffer?

The priest cautions her sternly against piling up more sin. She, poor creature, conceived without the blessing of the church, a bastard, must learn to keep her head down, listen to her mother, before it is too late and her soul is eternally damned, cast into the pit. After he is gone, deep in the stone basement, she cries out over and over, but there is no sound. No one to hear.

Over time Ofelia gives all her money to the church. And in some unholy pact, when she dies, she gives the church her virgin daughter, kept prisoner for them all these years. But still the stain will not wash out. This stain so innocently acquired! Ofelia had been so young, so wealthy, and so full of her own beauty.

Rome in 1920; what a place to be young and rich and beautiful! The parties, the art, the romance. And Duke Leone Caetani was the most perfect forbidden fruit. What began with vanity and lust led to a long list of unforgivable sins that followed, year upon year, as simply as walking into a trap; the gate thrown shut by the darkly-hooded priests and by the righteous, clacking tongues of Rome's high society. Thrown out. Excommunicated. Sentenced to the ends of the earth. Forever.

The priest, in the attic room, rolled the words like marbles in his mouth, but there was no way to forgive the sins that kept piling up. This is the stain, indelible and dark, that covers every surface of the house like a thin, grey layer of ash. Ofelia cannot touch living flesh. She has a horror of it. If she touches flesh, the smell is like electricity burning skin. After the touching and the burning, the ash filters down and the air is difficult to breathe. When the priest leaves, she washes her hands up to the elbows. She scrubs the ash off the table and the floor. Cleaned. Everything must be cleaned.

She watches her child grow in the image of the father: those same long limbs, that same inquisitive mind. The father, Leone, who ruined her life, whom she loved! Who abandoned her, in his death, to this place where only the church and the trunks in the basement smell of Rome. And the rest is the horror of distance. The endless train ride across the empty plains had numbed her already, when the endless mountains crushed her. Her soul withered and shrank as she realised the immensity of her transgression, measured against the lonely miles from civilisation. Even the gentle lapping summers of our bucolic valley only intensified the pain. She is flung out by Rome and she will never be warm again. The cause: this bastard child who had forced her sins to the light of day. And see how the child grows like the father! But what had been handsome in the father is homely in the daughter, awkward. Her feet will never fit any of the dainty shoes. The girl is messy with mother's sin.

And Ofelia's wall shimmers and becomes dark and liquid. She wanders down shadowy hallways and hears spiteful whispering behind closed doors. She hears the clacking tongues of Rome. She raises herself, stands straight and stiff against the gossip; she shakes her head, fingers her rosary beads and fixes her eye upon the distance. Her face is narrow and pinched. Her eyes are hard and black. The dark clouds come rolling in and through the turbulent mists she sees the pictures. They come and go. Speak and are silent. And she sees her daughter, in the garden, dreaming of freedom and love. She smashes her fist through the pictures of dancing, of kissing, the sighs of love! She smashes her dark, watery mirror and wakes screaming, shivering from the mists. "My heart! My heart!" she cries and little Miss Juule comes running with warm towels. The girl must stand before Mother and confess these horrid thoughts. There is no denying. Mother's eyes cut right through, as hard as chipped glass.

"I was not to leave the house anymore. I was not to go into the garden anymore. She had seen my lust, she said. I would go to hell, that was certain. I must confess to the priest immediately. The priest said I should be punished most severely. And I was.

"After that it was ten long years I suffocated under her eye, writhed in guilt for my evil soul, hated myself for the hatred I felt. I died over and over and I lay all night, eyes wide open, under a layer of thin, grey ash. Worst of all, I could no longer cry. My mouth and eyes were plugged with ash."

◆ ◆ ◆

Mother died in 1960. Finally, after twenty-five years, the gates opened and the world flooded in. And our Countess, aged forty-two, stepped, timidly, into the free street.

◆ ◆ ◆

The year was 1966 and I was still living at home, in my last year of high school. Our Countess was preparing to give a night school course on the history of art. My father made slides of statues from her books to show in the course. We set up the screen to see the slides. After we'd seen a few slides our Countess became very upset with the idea of a public showing.

"They will think this is pornography, smut, filth. They will not understand that this is art," she said, and she gestured toward the perfect penis of Michaelangelo's David. Her voice became very high, verging on hysteria. I said,

"What do you mean?" and she said

"They are Canadians. They are not cultured. They will not understand," and she wailed like she was going to be crucified.

Those gods, those statues belonged to her alone during those long years of imprisonment and she was afraid to share them with the common rabble. She was a sinner to long so badly for love, to take these statues to her heart, with the words of great poets to serenade the communion. She was a sinner for her dreams. And she did not want to share her beautiful, warm sin with the world.

She got a job teaching at the Catholic School and she went to all the Masses. One Sunday she had a special chance to go out on the ranges with some friends. She had a chance for an adventure. She said to the priest, "I hope it won't be too much to ask if I can miss this one Sunday, for this opportunity." And the priest said, "Well, if you feel you can put your love of God behind a picnic then let your conscience be your guide."

So she did. She went with her friends into the hills and she quit the damn church. They had taken enough. Mother and Church. The church had all her money, every cent. Mother had made certain of that. All those years looking after her, her slave, and she was left penniless.

Our Countess went away to university and became a teacher. She got a driver's license and became a menace on the road. She loved the speed, headlong into oblivion. She was intoxicated with her freedom, flying through the countryside, summer and winter. Accident after accident! And broken bones beyond count. They were a joke of the freedom. The pain was freedom-pain and she loved it.

And the energy, where did it come from? She would get up at five o'clock in the morning and paint those huge scapes. Possessed by the visions. Painting to her own rules of proportion and colour. The shimmering ghost of her father leading her deeper and deeper into the inferno. The Gods were unleashed! She would drive, breakneck speed, eight o'clock in the morning, 20 miles to Lumby, to teach. She would teach all day with an uncommon passion. Teach these backwoods urchins she had taken to her heart. These were her children, to fill her barren womb. These were all the possible children stolen from her.

"Poetry will save the world. Art will bring us home. Science will find noble inventions for mankind," she implored.

"Use your talents. Think: God gave you a brain. Just because you are born in a backwater doesn't mean you have to be backward." She was a thunderbolt.

Lumby is a village, smaller than our little town, and even more parochial. Lumby is a logging town, and our Countess brought culture with a passion that was bred in the bone and fermented in a sealed casket for 25 years.

There is no surprise in the way our Countess died. She breathed deeply, in her glory years of freedom, but the damage was already done. Like a miner, she had been breathing bad air for too long. And like a miner, she had surfaced with precious metals and stones from another world. But, even in death, Mother was still hanging around in that big house, infecting the air, squeezing the life out of our Countess. Jealous of any pleasure. When our Countess became sick, Mother was a malignant presence beside her bed. A deadly spectre hovered over the room.

The last winter our Countess was alive, she came to my mother's home for dinner on Christmas Eve. We had to carry her up the steps and make a ramp over the snow to get her into the house. She was still so magnificently tall and heavy, even in a wheelchair. We had a great time that evening, laughing and talking, and our Countess was happy to be in the middle of life.

The last few years she had become a prisoner in that house again. Her legs were wrapped in bandages to hide the sores. She spent most of her time in one room, staring at the ceiling. But on Christmas Eve, our Countess had a sip of sherry and ate a little cake. That evening, my mother made a special gift, to me, of a lead-glass decanter that had been in our family for a long time. I placed the decanter on the carpet between my mother and myself. Our Countess was laughing at something that my little sister had said and the slender neck of the decanter shattered, as if by some internal pressure. The lead-glass stop was blown out and landed on the carpet a foot away. The decanter fell over and lay on its side, the top of the fluted neck a jagged ring. No one had touched the decanter. No door had opened to let in a breeze. Our Countess stopped laughing and she said, "That is Mother. She is angry because I am enjoying myself."

From beyond the grave Mother kept a steady pressure

on her daughter. She pressed down with her hands on our Countess's chest. She wanted to defeat this ungracious lust for life, to destroy this brilliance that had created a complete cosmology to survive a journey through hell. Our Countess was already dying childless, a virgin, but that was not enough. Ofelia was affronted by this indulgence of paint, incensed by this conceit of poetry.

    I have the decanter, in a cabinet downstairs, and I treasure it even more now that it is broken. The lead-glass stop sits on the window sill in the kitchen, and makes prisms across the countertops in the late afternoon sun.

Aphid & The Rocket Lawnchair

Aphid, minor cult figure, founder and leader of the late, great, glandular rock band "Little Aphid and the Lymph Nodes" hummed softly down Pleasant Valley Road with his right hand on the steering wheel of his Buick '66. The interior of the car was a montage of week-old bananas, half-eaten burgers, ripped vinyl and, soaked permanently into the seat, just a hint of rancid baby puke.

Aphid's left hand was up his nose. The job seemed to require intense concentration and a deep commitment. A spiritual quest for a booger. To his credit, he wasn't eating them.

Priscilla, the myopic terror of the blue-rinse set, could barely see over the steering wheel of her Nash Rambler, even with two cushions under her. She was driving down sixty-five years of Memory Lane. She drove right through the stop sign at the corner of Pleasant Valley Road. She smashed into the driver's side of Aphid's Buick. Aphid's forefinger was driven like a spike into his brain. That forefinger smashed through his eyeball right into the king of boogers.

Priscilla was sitting very quietly, the imprint of her head

etched in the windshield. They took Aphid away in an ambulance with his finger strapped to his nose. They took Priscilla away in the ambulance with Aphid. Side by side off they went.

Priscilla's knee-high nylons were unravelling and she would not lie down. She sat stolidly, smoothing her mauve chiffon dress over her knees. Stolidly and silently she sat and Aphid talked on and on in a nasal drone.

That fateful spring Sunday. When Priscilla, dreaming a psalm for the Sunday school class she taught year-in and year-out, sang loud and off-key, floating down the hedge-lined lane:

Oh little children Come all ye hither

she sang, dressed in her best lilac scent. And Aphid, slightly stoned on the rank odours in his car, made a tune all mingling in the key of E. Mixing spring fragrance from outside, wafting hopeful and renewed through the window, he breathed deeply and sang high and clear:

Oh spring and lust and life as fecund now
as ever shall be!

and then he sang the inside odours, low and rasping:

stale winter crust of moldy bread and puke
and piss and cum as dull as duty.

So Aphid sang and Priscilla sang, each oblivious as stop signs, right onto the scalpel of Doctor Cameron.

Doctor Cameron loved to operate on Sunday. He was most creative on Sundays. His scalpel sang through flesh on Sundays. The quiet humm of the operating room and his faithful nurse of forty years handing him his hammers and chisels and saws. Slap slap precision.

Doctor Cameron deliberated whether to remove the

forefinger from Aphid's nose and risk a hemorrhage or leave the finger where it was, since the patient seemed to be chatting on quite happily. He chose the latter and amputated the forefinger. He then sutured the finger into Aphid's left nostril with a dozen beautiful butterfly stitches.

He was overcome with the freedom of Sunday in this small town, in this backward country, in this tiny hospital with only his trusted nurse of forty years to witness. He turned the music up. He began to sing. His nurse looked at him with adoring eyes. She remembered the old days together. They had been gods. Choosing, not only life and death, but the kinds of life and death. How beautiful it had been. To watch the victims die was not so beautiful as to watch them suffer the new, twisted life the Doctor gave them.

As soon as Dr. Cameron had finished with Aphid, in the joy and warmth of the moment, he operated on Priscilla. He drilled tiny holes in her forehead to relieve the pressure. Through the tiny holes he administered shocks. He prescribed psychotropic drugs and committed her to his own special ward.

He pronounced both operations a resounding success and went home to eat wild pheasant he shot in the orchard behind his country mansion. The nurse went home to her austere apartment in town. She walked down the hill, as usual, but once at home she drank a glass of sherry and smoked a cigarette. Both the nurse and the doctor spoke English with no trace of an accent. As if they had come from nowhere.

✦ ✦ ✦

One evening, shortly after his release from hospital, Aphid

was walking down a maple-lined sidewalk. He was a sight to see, bandaged about the nose and patched over his eye. His other eye straining in the socket, searching for some familiar shape and finding none. His mind was in a tenuous state. He was plagued with inner voices burrowing like worms through his Grey matter. A din of nonsense phrases, of mad accusations, of demands and commands resounded in his skull. Cutting through this noise the deep voice of an old man sounded clear and strong, like a trumpet. The handsome voice of the old man said,

"Rockets are good. They are dreams and youth and fascination and fear.

They sigh softly of what we long for and roar with the pain of our discontent."

Aphid spun around trying to catch a glimpse of this new voice. He only had one good eye. He spun around so fast he got dizzy and sat down with a plunk on the boulevard. The night was suddenly very quiet. He leaned against a tree trunk and blinked up at the sky. The night inside his head was quiet. Only the beautiful voice of the old man remained. The voice said, "Listen to the music, you idiot." And sure enough, Aphid could hear strains of music from the waterfront.

His old band, The Lymph Nodes, was playing down at the packing house and his friend, Bear, was blowing the harp and singing a popular song. The harp sound wove its way through the trees to Aphid. Then Bear was singing. He changed the words of the song to suit himself; head back he howled:

If I had a rocket lawnchaaair.
If I had a rocket lawnchaaair.
If I had a rocket lawnchaaair, I'd sail away.

At this precise moment, Aphid's forefinger twitched like the hind leg of a sleeping dog chasing rabbits. Perhaps it was the old man's voice in his skull. Perhaps it was the rocket song floating on the breeze. Perhaps it was the moon rising over the distant blue hills. Perhaps, perhaps, but unseen forces were yanking the tendons in Aphid's finger and making that finger jump.

Aphid's forefinger twitched and stroked his mushy grey matter. Rockets went off in his head and the soothing voice of the dead science fiction writer spooked him from his blind side. This was the historical moment. This was the moment when Aphid's Forefinger became a lightning rod, connecting him to the spirit world.

In later years, "twitching like Aphid's Forefinger" became a folk saying in our little valley. It meant different things to different people. To the religious folk, and that was most of the population, it meant dancing with the devil. But to them, everything meant dancing with the devil.

That moment, sitting on the grass with his back against a big maple tree and a cathedral sky calling him, Aphid knew he must build A Rocket Lawnchair. The popular rocket song drifted through the trees like bees. Diagrams wandered through Aphid's head as if he were turning the pages of a book. He could see the whirling umbrella-propella above; The Chair with wide comfortable wooden arms and built-in drink holders. The drink with a small umbrella of its own. And below, he could hear the engines making music, to defy gravity. How very pleasant the ride would be, cushioned on those notes.

From a distance The Rocket Lawnchair would look like a flying cherry against the sky.

✦ ✦ ✦

Later that spring evening, that fateful evening when his forefinger first twitched, Aphid stole the rowboat that lay upsidedown on the beach beside the old packing house.

Down the lake he went. The oars splash splash in the dark water. Bear, standing on the balcony of the packing house, said he could see the flash of oars in the moonlight. And he said the silence was intense after the noise of the party. Way out in the lake the steady rhythm of the oars stopped. Bear could hear Aphid bailing water from the leaking boat. Then, once again, the oars splash splash into the darkness.

Aphid set up camp way down the lake. Nobody lived down there. He was all alone with the lapping water and the sky. Late at night he would row into town and take a few things. Things began to disappear all over town. Weird stuff that nobody really cared about. Things to hold things together. Wide flat things. Round, smooth objects. He was both random and particular in his choices.

One night Aphid stole from Nasty Horace. Stingy Horace. Peg-leg Horace, with his curtains always drawn: busy filing lawsuits against his neighbours. Horace, whose only companion was his withered mother rocking in the darkened room covered in blankets. His father long dead. Horace was a young man who seemed old because of his pale wrinkled skin, wooden leg and bad temper. He only came out in spring to kill the dandelions. He clomped down the front steps, swinging that leg, with the canister full of DDT already strapped to his back and the hose in his hand. He loved to inject poison into the dandelion roots and watch them wither. Then he climbed stiffly back up the stairs and closed the door and left the spring to us.

When Horace slept he placed his wooden leg beside his bed. Aphid stole it. He didn't take the easy money hidden in bundles throughout the house. He only took The Leg.

The morning sight of Horace bolting from his house, swinging his stump furiously down the hill. The village roused by his cries,

"My leg, my leg, he's stolen my leg," Horace yelled all the way to the police station.

From behind his desk Constable Duncan ram-rod straight, as always, asked the appropriate questions and filed the appropriate report.

Constable Duncan lived in the red brick house a few blocks from the station. He walked out every morning straight as an arrow. Clean as a pin. He left his sluttish wife in her slovenly bed. The cats to dine on leftover scraps on the counters. Dishes, boxes, clutter everywhere, dust and dirt in archeological layers on every horizontal surface. And Constable Duncan, the military man, walked out, shiny and new, every morning.

Everywhere, except in the red brick house, Constable Duncan was the law. He was a good man. He was a fair man. And he made out the report for leg-theft with only a hint of laughter hidden behind his waxed mustache.

❖ ❖ ❖

Aphid was down the lake. He studied at night with a coal oil lamp, hanging from a tree, and his drawings spread out on a picnic table stolen from the town park. Aphid had dragged the table half a mile to the shore of the lake. He'd loaded the table across the bow of the boat and rowed, wallowing and top heavy, with the water lapping inches from death, down the lake. The cold water was flat as a mirror. No breeze stirred. Most unusual for this early season. Not until Aphid was safely on the shore, up to his knees in the water, scrambling over the rough gravel, did the spring breezes resume their play over the wide water.

He dragged the table up the beach to the meadow's edge. No sooner was he seated under a big fir tree than the wind began rocking the lamp that hung from the lowest branch and whipping up the deadly whitecaps on the water.

The lamp had been donated by Fisher's Hardware. Aphid had spent hours at the little store discussing the intricacies of his visionary project and complaining of the long dark nights with no light to work by.

A contribution was inevitable. The lamp, a supply of coal oil, nuts and bolts, pliers and screwdrivers, were all donated. The Fisher brothers gave freely. Otherwise, Aphid might spend the night, curled up on the floor beside the old wood stove, talking crazy in his sleep.

✦ ✦ ✦

I met Aphid when he stole my lumber. He stole it piece by piece, night after night. The dogs didn't bark; they licked him and rolled over to have their bellies scratched. The geese, usually so alert to any intruder, didn't make a sound. Neither did the ducks. Not a quack. I watched from my window as he made his way up the creek. He was walking in the water, going against the current, and pulling the boat behind him with a rope wrapped around his chest. His plan was to steal my wood and float quietly back down the creek to the lake. He succeeded, night after night. And I watched. And he knew I watched and I knew he knew.

It is because I knew he knew and he knew I knew and we both smiled at each other across the night (as he loaded my lumber into his boat) that so many things happened. How can you see a smile across a hundred yards in the moonless night? You can't. But I did. I saw him smile clear and bright as day. And he saw me smile, and he saw me raise my hand in a sign of peace.

Poor old Priscilla, finally released from Doctor Cameron's Special Ward, wandered aimless and forlorn down those maple streets. Beneath the trees she felt safe from the unblinking eye of the sky. The Special Ward had been a terrible place. She had been unable to move. Unable to scream. Suspended above herself in disembodied terror, gasping in a hostile air. The clinical faces swimming by, poking at her with needles. She would stay close to the earth now. Go to ground and lick her wounds. She would stay beneath the trees.

She had been a teacher before the accident. Both at Sunday school, with the little ones, and during the week at high school. And now they had relieved her of her duties. She loved poetry and she recited the beautiful fragments of the great poems that she could still remember. But it was true, she could not remember all the names of all the poets and she had forgotten so many poems she once knew. Nonetheless, she was of value as a teacher and she would prove herself.

She would go to the principal, textbooks in hand. She would make him take her back. She loved to teach, especially young people at this rude age of adolescence when they were, simultaneously, so self absorbed and so idealistic.

She entered the school. She rustled like leaves in wind down the hall. You would not believe a person so round could move so lightly. No wooden board creaked beneath her feet. The secretary, in the hall outside the principal's office, did not see her go by. Priscilla opened the door to the principal's office so perfectly the hinges didn't squeak. The breeze did not blow through. It was as if she had not opened the door at all.

She stood for a moment and watched the principal. He didn't see her. He opened the bottom drawer of his desk (where he kept a cane), took a flask from beneath a stack of papers, uncorked with his teeth and drank heartily. Priscilla said, "Good morning Larry, you old lush." Larry choked and spat the whisky across his desk. "Yes, Larry, it's a fine morning for a drink," she said and grabbed the flask from his hand and took a swig and spat it across his desk, just as he had done. "When in Rome do as the Romans do," she said. "Is spitting whisky a new custom? Some fad I have missed during my incarceration?" "Oh God," the principal thought, "that same mauve dress. That same blue hair. Those same square shoes and big white pearls. Those same thick glasses. But there is something very different . . . " He said nothing.

Priscilla continued, "I have known you since you were a little boy, Larry. And you always were a little weasel. I want to come back to teach. You will help me because I know so many nasty things about you. You started young, don't you remember? At seven years old, five dead cats in the washing machine. At eleven, the barn burnt to the ground. And at fifteen, you little bastard," and she gave him such a look and shook her head slowly back and forth, "but we don't talk about that, do we?" she asked, "and when do I start teaching?" she asked again.

"You can start tomorrow," the principal smiled weakly. "You seem perfectly fine to me, Miss Priscilla."

❖ ❖ ❖

Tomorrow, unfortunate tomorrow.

In our country, spring is a time when the perfect calm of a clear blue day can be shattered by the power of a wayward storm thrashing through our village out of nowhere. Before the tempest the stagnant air is saturated with electricity. Then come whirling winds and stabbing lightning, followed by thunder and driving rain. The turbulence lasts only an hour or so and then the sky is blue once more, the air is calm and peace is restored. If not for the damp ground and a few broken branches, we might think it all a dream.

Tomorrow was a day like this.

Pricsilla walked to class beneath the late spring apple blossoms in the early morning sun. She chose her path carefully and when she was forced to cross a treeless expanse, she ran. She covered her head and when she reached the safety of trees, she rested. She sat very still and felt the roots beneath her digging down and the water inside the trunk rising up. And the textures of the bark were alive against her back. And so she went from tree to tree and then a final dash across the school lawns.

The class went quite well. She had her notes so she

wouldn't forget. But at two o'clock in the afternoon the storm came up. A storm that broke big branches from old trees. That laid old trees to the ground. That flooded creek beds and storm sewers. This was a storm whose bolts burned buildings to the ground. Lightning thudded into the earth right outside the schoolhouse.

Remember, the good doctor had drilled holes inside Priscilla's skull, administered electric shocks, played music directly into her brain. Kept her asleep for days on end. Changed her diaper like a baby. How long had she been gone? A day a week a year? She couldn't tell.

"How long is forever in hell?" she said to the nurse, as she was bathed and dressed and walked to the door.

"How long?" she said plaintive as a bird crying in the dusk. The nurse replied,

"Two weeks, that is all. Just two weeks," in a voice as flat and cold as steel plate.

And now she was teaching and the electric storm raged outside the schoolhouse and the children, frozen to their seats, watched as Priscilla's face was obscured by a swirling mist of sparks. The sparks came out of the charged air, out of nothing, and disappeared into her skull through the holes. She seemed very calm in the midst of all this swirling. You might be tempted to say she looked "beatific".

"I have come to realize," she said to the awestruck class in a voice smooth and soft, "that I must go." She gave a dramatic pause, her head a halo of sparks. "Oh you will see," she said serenely, "you will see," and she laughed. "You will do things and things will be done to you. You will be rich or poor, and then you will be old and nothing will make any sense. And then, if you have been deepened by living, you will understand poetry, which is about love and the loss of love and beauty and horror. And then you will die. And if you are stupid you will forget about seeing and feeling and your heart will dry up to the size of a pea and you will become 'The Walking Dead'."

She finished her speech and climbed on the chair, and from the chair onto the desk top. She spread her arms and looked intensely at the class. There was no sound but the crackle of electricity in the air. "I hereby sentence you to life," she proclaimed above the clashing thunder. And down she jumped and off she ran down the hall and out into the summer storm and out of the school board's disdain, forevermore. The class remained seated.

Priscilla ran and hid beneath the trees and Aphid found her there, curled like a fallen leaf. She was not cold because she was so full of electricity. The rain drops hissed on her skin. And when the storm had passed, Aphid put her in his rowboat and took her down the lake to his camp.

And that is how Priscilla came to stay with Aphid. Aphid, who loved to dream of The Rocket Lawnchair. Who talked about flying all day and night. Who stole and schemed to build a flying machine. And Priscilla, afraid of the sky.

✦ ✦ ✦

The stolen leg of Horace stood on the stolen picnic table in the middle of Aphid's camp. The leg was made of walnut wood. Every night Horace had rubbed it with oils to keep it from splitting. Now the wood was dark and lustrous.

The top of the leg was fitted with a padded leather pouch to hold the stump. The middle of the leg, the knee, was made with two metal hinges that locked and required the occupant to kick the leg violently forward at every step. The bottom of the leg was riveted with brass to protect the wood when striking the pavement.

Aphid had mounted the leg on a salvaged record player and he spun it around to admire the possibilities. He was deep in thought and muttering under his breath. Priscilla was still sleeping.

The day had dawned and a mist rose over the lake. Not a sound but the ducks way out in the water laughing at the mist rising in slender streams, disappearing into the sun. Behind Aphid, through the rising mists, the rudiments of The Rocket Lawnchair could be seen. Even in this early stage of construction you could see it was a place to sit in comfort. A padded chair with reclining capabilities. A chair to absorb the shocks of flight. There was a gyroscopic feel to the shining aluminum tubes that ran around the chair. The tubes that Aphid called, "Heavenly Rolling Bars".

The Lawnchair was suspended by ropes between two fir trees at the edge of the camp. Aphid could pull the ropes and send the armchair spinning: like ringing the bells in a church steeple.

Priscilla slept and slept. So tired she was. She would wake with tiny eyes blinking against the light and drink the soup that Aphid brought. Aphid holding her head. Slurp, slurp she went. Poor little pale thing. Happy to have the scented cedar boughs to sleep on and the goosedown quilt to cover. The little bivouac overhead in case of rain. The birch trees all around. She could hear the birch trees singing while she slept. She dreamt the birch trees were beautiful white goddesses dancing around her. They sang feminine secrets and shone intensely white in the moonlight. They shook their branches over her head and from the branches fell little droplets of water that cooled her body. And she was safe, breathing in the cedar scent.

Maybe it was the moon rising over the hill? Maybe it was the dreadful holes in her skull? Maybe it was the mists? Maybe it was just a dream? Then it was morning and time to get up. The mists were gone, eaten by the sun. And she could hear Aphid talking to himself. Or maybe he was speaking to that horrid leg, spinning on the picnic table?

✦ ✦ ✦

Constable Duncan was reluctant to mount an expedition down the lake to capture The Leg. Horace was furious. His anger was easy to understand; he had no leg.

Horace spent his evenings writing letters to the local paper. He spent his days pointing his finger at Constable Duncan and bending any ear to his plight. Mind you, how much of a loss was that awful leg? Every step an angry jolt of locking hinges, a spine-shuddering thud of wood on pavement. The tender skin of the stump worn raw rubbing against that ill-conceived pouch.

Horace had endured that torture for years. And why? Because he wanted to wear long pants with two legs like everybody else. Two pant legs that dropped right to the ground. And so every day he suffered and everyone he encountered must suffer with him. Suffer his DDT in springtime, his lawsuits all year round, his spiteful stare and pursed lips frowning on every innocent act. He especially hated children. All that running and jumping and laughing.

At home, behind closed curtains, Horace never wore that goddamned leg. He glided smoothly on his one leg from room to room. His balance was impeccable.

Sometimes he used a cane. Sometimes he used a crutch. Sometimes he used neither and bounded like a deer around the house, ricocheting happily off the walls. But he never left the house without strapping on that painful leg. Never in the public eye.

Now, with his leg stolen, his life changed. That first furious walk down the hill had exposed his secret. In the wink of an angry eye he had bounded out the door and down the road yelling, "My leg, my leg, he's stolen my leg," at the top of his lungs. And in that thoughtless instant his life changed.

"How nimble he is," the widow lady, hanging her wash in the early morning hush, noted with a raised eyebrow. "How strong his one leg!" the little boys admired, struck to silence by the bounding spectacle. The news spread fast. Those who had seen the event were proud to tell the story from their own perspective,

"Flew right over my head."

"Like a kangaroo bounding past my window."

"Damn near knocked me over," they wagged and nodded all up and down the street. Soon, around town, Horace was known as an athlete. A competitor in a field of his own. And even while he ranted against Aphid and cried in the papers over the loss of his leg. Even while he spent hours in the library studying the law as it pertained to his situation. He could not help himself; he was happy. He loved to glide down the streets with his unique method of locomotion. A combination hop, glide, slide and jump. He used trees and walls and fences to ricochet like a pin ball down the street. And he loved the admiration of the town. He was free at last to dance in public. Free at last from that awful leg.

But the Mayor spoke to Constable Duncan. "Something must be done," he said. "Horace is not the only person filing complaints. There is the widow, whose goosedown quilt was stolen from her clothesline the same day as The Leg disappeared. And the widow's pig is missing, stolen.

"And the aluminum tubes, specially made for my circular staircase, very expensive, imported from the east, stolen from my fenced backyard. My damn Doberman dogs didn't make a peep. Silent as lambs. And my new swivel chair, built to fit and very expensive, stolen as well. The insurance company is demanding receipts." The mayor wrung his hands together. He was worried about those receipts.

"Aphid has stolen it all," he sighed. "This has gone too far and must be stopped," and he pounded his thin fist on the desktop. And Constable Duncan replied,

"I have no proof that it was Aphid who stole those things. And even if I did have proof I have no boat because there is no money for a boat."

Constable Duncan did not whisper under his breath that the mayor was a thieving bastard stealing from the village. He did not whisper because he was a military man and they are taught never to whisper under their breath.

And so, for a time, Aphid and Priscilla were left to themselves, way down the lake. Nobody came to visit.

❖ ❖ ❖

Perhaps you have never spent a long time in the woods when nobody comes to visit. And perhaps you have not endured such horrible surgeries as Aphid and Priscilla. I pray you have never encountered a surgeon named Dr. Cameron and his faithful nurse. But our village has.

Dr. Cameron liked our village the moment he laid eyes upon it, so many years ago. He liked the isolation. In those days we lived a long way away.

North of the village there was mile upon mile of steep valleys. The forests were thick. The winters were harsh and the summers were short. Few travelers came from the north. And if a traveler came from the east or west he must cross many high mountain ranges through narrow passes. In some places the snow never melted. To the south, our gentle hills gave way to an immense desert and beyond the desert there was a race of people we did not understand. And our village was at the confluence of these geographies. We rested in the swales of a gentle sloping valley: at the place where the forest turns to grassland and the grassland turn back to forest. We were the spot on the map where all the breezes joined together, each breeze taking power in its season, but softened by the others. So our weather was changeable, but mostly pleasant.

The village was situated on a hillside and an active person could climb to the top of Black Rock Hill and stand at the cliff's edge and survey the whole village in a single glance.

From clifftop, at your feet, small farms stretched out in a patchwork of orchards and pastures, and beyond them, the upper end of Main Street began its descent to the water's edge. First, the street ran wide and majestic past the big houses at the top of the hill. Then the big houses gave way to modest homes and the street fell like a gentle roller coaster down the hillside. And at the bottom of the hill the street crossed over the tracks and passed beside the red brick station. From the tracks, Main Street descended gently to the lake.

At the end of Main Street, thrust out into the lake, the old packing house stood trembling on timber legs that descended into the crusty depths. In the olden days the paddlewheel steamers rubbed against those timber legs, and the wagons rumbled up and down Main Street carrying apples to and fro. The lake was turquoise blue in the daylight and black as train oil in the night.

And in between the train tracks and the lakeshore were little shops hidden safely beneath the big maple trees. The shopkeepers, hopeful for customers from land or water, stood behind the counters or arranged merchandise on the shelves or idled outside beneath their signs. The signs of these shops were half-obscured by the budding green leaves. The shop windows were framed by the sturdy branches. The little shops were built from rough lumber, the floors were rough planks and the basements flooded with every storm.

Halfway between the tracks and the lake was The Government Building. The Government Building was right in the middle of the village, pride of the community, built with granite blocks hauled on barges from the quarry down the lake. And there was marble, imported from Italy, in black and white squares on the floor. And brass cages and oak desks as heavy as the ages.

Behind the government building there was a park to honour the war dead. A pretty little park with a high stone wall curving along the front and a wrought-iron gate. There was a path winding up a little hill to the granite monument where the names were inscribed. The pathway was lined with huge blue spruce trees and the same trees spread majestically across the park lawns.

Across the street from the government building, in two

directions, were the hotels. On the north-east corner there was the Grande Hotel: spelled with the extra "e" for a continental flavour. The Grande Hotel looked like a big shoebox. Downstairs the bar. Upstairs the rooms. Toilet and bath at the end of the corridor and the fire escape out the bathroom window. Never take a room in the middle of the shoebox. The fire escape is too far to run when a drunken spark lights up the wood-framed walls. The walls filled with wood shavings for insulation, dry as a popcorn fart. Poof, a pile of ashes. There was nothing grand about The Grande Hotel. The Great Fire killed all the bedbugs.

And on the south-east corner was The Coldwater Hotel, a ramshackle agglomeration with additions from every era since the beginning of our history. Each generation had added another layer of stucco over wood, or wood over wallpaper. Each time their was a population boom, or even the hint that there might be a population boom, new rooms were added. If a person knew where to look, the entire history of the village could be seen inside that dilapidated labyrinth of rooms.

There were ghosts in the beer parlour from the turn of the century stealing drinks from the paying customers, winking and laughing at each other across the smoky room, ready to mount up in the morning and skeedaddle up to the Cariboo. There were guests in the attic rooms that would never leave. They spent their days gazing out the windows, peering through the maple branches to the street below. And, of course, there were the giant maple trees, bending the light through a lace of wood and foliage, silent witnesses to human folly.

That was the centre of town: the government building, two hotels and a park. Below that centre there was Lower

Town, for the working classes. Above that centre there was Upper Town, for the wealthier folk. The street that ran through the middle of town, intersecting Main Street in a perfect cross, was called Church Street.

Oh tiny village with thirty-six churches! And thirty-six priests and preachers and ministers vying to save the souls of that village. And thirty-six congregations all up and down Church Street.

Sunday morning on Church Street was a feast of religions. There were the established faiths, of course, but there were also the new denominations invented in basements and backyards. There were congregations of ten brave souls and, sometimes, congregations of only one, pitiful soul.

A lonely priest deserted by his congregation was a sorry sight, clinging to his vision, like a drowning man on a packing crate in the middle of an ocean. Congregations could be as fickle as harlots and were often denounced as such by the preachers, exhorting their sheep to stay in the fold. Nonetheless, sometimes entire congregations deserted en masse, and swarmed to a new spiritual hive.

The Catholics were on Church Street with their formidable edifice, indisputably the most grand. The Anglicans, with their graceful steeple and separate bell tower, gave no ground to Rome. The United Church, solid, square, expensive and noncommittal, sat mid-ground in between. Those were The Big Three of religion and then there were all the rest, spread out along the avenue like smaller fishes, thrashing in the turbulent waters of the New World.

There was The Greek Orthodox and The Russian Orthodox and The Slavic Alliance for Jesus and The Elim Tabernacle and The Seventh Day Adventist and The

Jehovah's Witness and The Church Of God and The Church Of The Alliance of All Faiths and The People's Church and The First and Third Baptist and The Pentecostal and The Lutheran and The Presbyterian and The Reformed Lutheran and The Mormon and The Methodist and the Christadelphian and so many others rising on a crest of popularity and descending quickly into obscurity.

Never has their been such a contest for souls. The preachers sang their hearts out. Competition was stiff beneath the giant trees that shaded Church Street from end to end.

✦ ✦ ✦

Lower Town. The sidestreets of Lower Town were lined with little houses and in between the houses were woodlands with little creeks running through. And all the little houses were shaded by the woodland trees. The sun was never too hot beneath their canopy. The storms could not penetrate between the mighty trunks. Beneath their branches the streets were safe. Only the wealthy dared to live on the barren hillside above the trees. At the very bottom of the hill, in the smallest houses, lived the Ukrainians.

The Ukrainians ate apples and potatoes and turnips from their root cellars. They ate Kolbassa that hung from the rafters. They made vodka from the potatoes grown in the backyard and they slept happy. Why not? They had traveled a long way and they were tired. They were happy that nobody hated them enough to kill them. Life was good in this new country.

In that long ago spring, the young Doctor Cameron, just

arrived from God-knows-where, woke the Ukrainians from their winter's sleep. "Come work for me," he said, offering twice the usual wage. He wanted to build a private hospital behind Black Rock Hill. "To serve the people of the village," he said over and over.

The men were happy to sweat the winter fat from their bodies. To stink the spring air with their farts. They shouted lies to each other about the famous fucking they did all winter, as they dug the heavy clay with picks. The younger boys were shy with all this talk of tits and cunts and the smell of fishes and the men made coarse gestures behind their backs and the work was very hard for them. The men called the young boys "girls" and laughed at them. When they started digging it was early spring and the wild sunflowers were coming into bloom. And when they were finished it was late summer and the wasps attacked their lunches.

They dug and dug, and built forms and poured concrete all summer long. The cheques were always on time. Every Friday was payday. The Doctor walked around handing out the cheques himself. He eyed the strong Ukrainian men up and down. The men were nervous when the Doctor's eye was on them. They kept their faces down and they did not laugh about sex. They crossed themselves and they were anxious to leave. They longed for the warm, plump women at home. They longed for the smells of baking bread and simmering soup, supper on the table. A place where they could be men again and forget the Doctor's eye.

◆ ◆ ◆

The village was far too busy on Sundays to hear the

screams. Besides, the walls of the laboratory were very thick concrete. Five church bells ringing, ten church organs wheezing, thirty-six holy men exhorting and choirs, choirs, choirs everywhere. Well, you understand, they could not hear the screams.

The beer parlours were closed on Sundays, of course, so even the most ravenous drunk could be herded onto Church Street, washed up and slicked down. Presentable in a ragged sort of way, but shivering in his uncontrollable desire to be somewhere else. Anywhere else, drinking and forgetting. The village was busy busy busy on Sundays. Busy dressing up for God.

And so, you see, Doctor Cameron loved his Sundays. On Sundays he owned the sunshine of spring and the falling rain of autumn and the blanket of snow in winter that muffled the unpleasant noises so well. Winter he loved the most. He often commented to his faithful nurse how quickly a blanket of snow absorbed the sound of pain. "And then," he sighed, "deathly silence, such a heavenly pleasure," and he turned to the nurse as they stood together in the doorway of the laboratory and watched the falling snow. The village was over the hill, hidden from view, and the private hospital looked down onto orchards and little farms as peaceful as Jesus in a manger.

Behind them, inside the basement laboratory, were corridors and corridors of sealed rooms. When you were inside a room the door was closed and they only brought you out to measure the length, breadth and width of your madness.

For years and years the town hummed away, as pretty as an apple, as turquoise as summer water. The experiments continued right beside the joyous fanning summers, hot as silk. The painful cries were muffled right outside the winter's hearth and cheer. The seasons flowed by and only a few people arrived in the village and only a few left. It seemed as if nothing would ever change. And why should it? This was a quiet little village cut off from the rest of the world. Lazy as rattlesnakes in summer and snuggled beneath snow, with nothing but a few sleepy streams of smoke ascending to the sky in winter.

But that was years ago. Time has forgot. And there is nothing left but broken concrete, if you know where to look.

Aphid and Priscilla came to town. Priscilla had a pension cheque. Aphid had sweet fuck all. Splash splash they went down the lake in the bright turquoise water. Aphid rowing and Priscilla bailing. They didn't come right into town but pulled the stolen boat ashore secretly and walked the last mile. Aphid promised he wouldn't steal anything.

Priscilla wagged her finger in his face and said, "No, no, no, you mustn't," always the schoolmarm.

Aphid replied head down, "I will not steal, not even camembert cheese." False promises.

They came to town on a Monday morning in late spring. Something was wrong. The village was always lethargic on Mondays, the citizens having expended their energy so lavishly appeasing the Sunday Gods.

But not this Monday. City work trucks roared up and down Main Street. Men shouted orders to each other. Chainsaws howled. Blind John Brown, The Foreman Of Public Works, glared and peered down the tunnels of his blurred vision and sweated big circles under his arms and down his back and over his big belly. He was directing traffic, but he was completely useless because he couldn't see a damn thing. His theory of management was: He who shouts the loudest and longest is boss. John yelled and waved his arms, his silver hard hat glistening in the sun. The world a wicked blur of potential disasters.

Blind John Brown hated the trees. The trees were wicked creatures who tripped him, sticking a root up through the ground and grabbing his toe most painfully. They lowered their branches and cracked him on his forehead knocking him flat on his arse. As a child he was too fat to climb the trees and the other boys threw chestnuts from the high branches. John waddled home all pissy pants and the other boys yelled, "Fat and blind. Fat and blind," from the treetops.

Now, John stood in the middle of the street pointing and puffing and enjoying his vengeance. The trees came crashing down. The chainsaws howled at his command.

The sound of saws sent Priscilla into the most dreadful state of panic. Trees being cut! Precious wooden flesh ripped to pieces. What to do? What to do? She ran ahead of Aphid into the street, and was almost hit by a truck full of maple branches. She was yelling and gasping and holding her head together with her hands. The unbearable sky was a gaping wound opening above her beloved street. Blue going on forever and blinding light burning into her skull. She needed shade to heal her wounds.

The branches seemed to be falling all around her in a gentle hail of green. Soft, so soft they fell and floated in the air like green tears and oh how she cried big blue tears. "My trees, My trees," she moaned and held her arms out in every direction at once.

And down at the lower end of Main Street the trunks were cut off, right down to the pavement. And poison was put in the wound so that not even the smallest shoot would sprout through. Spring had been shattered.

Aphid, too, ran sobbing up the street, snot streaming down his face, mixing with his tears. His one eye, all red and rheumy, searching the faces of the shopkeepers standing like sleepwalkers, arms crossed, in front of their stores. Searching for some meaning, some explanation.

Poor Aphid. Poor Priscilla. Poor stupid village. And poor poor maple trees.

✦ ✦ ✦

From the east, bulldozers were pushing through the mountains, braving the avalanches that thundered down the peaks. The new highway from the east was almost complete.

From the west, bulldozers pushed their way across the high plateau. The new highway from the west was almost complete.

New people would soon flood into the valley. The smell of money mixed with the dry odour of religion created a unique bouquet over the village. The sour smell of too much soap, too much scrubbing of the skin, could not eradicate the sweet smell of avarice oozing, unbidden, through the pores. And so the trees must go.

Order in Council it was. Progress they said. Too many leaves clogging the storm sewers. Falling branches a hazard; someone might be killed. Maple bugs falling on the tourists, how unpleasant. Wanton roots choking the foundations of buildings. All good reasons.

✦ ✦ ✦

Doctor Cameron was not happy about the new highways. He liked things the way they were. He was too old to start over. From the village he had a steady supply of accidental victims. You know the types: derelict drunks nobody missed too much. Retarded children nobody wanted. Depressed housewives that he cured in a couple of weeks. They went home in a permanent daze. They were never the same.

But the most desired material were bastard babies from teenage mothers. Sturdy genetic stuff for his own pleasure; not this mind-washing crap he must do for money.

The good doctor survived on a few small contracts from foreign governments. He got his work through friends from the good old days before The Fall. Old friends who had managed to land on their feet. But the work was repetitious, the bastards kept the good stuff for themselves. All he got was the crumbs they didn't want: brainwashing experiments, deprivation chambers, new drugs and poisons.

But the Doctor's real passion was genetics; that was the future. Genetics made his heart thump.

The pregnant families came to him with cap in hand, "Please doctor, can you help?" they pleaded and the doctor said, "I can find a home for the baby," and he called for the nurse and he whispered aside to the distraught parents, "She's a trusty old soul, heart of gold," and he pointed at the nurse as she entered the room and he winked in a friendly manner. Trusty old soul indeed.

"No shame, no shame," he said to the pregnant girl with

a warm, reassuring smile, a gentle hand on a sobbing shoulder. The family, so thankful, left bowing backwards out the door, cap still in hand. The young girl, sitting stiffly on the wooden chair, knees pressed firmly together, stayed.

The girl was treated like a princess and enjoyed the view from her private room. Delicious meals and music from speakers in the walls. So modern. She was flattered with the vitamins in tasty milkshakes. She was thankful for the discreet walks in the evening so as not to be seen. "Good for the baby," the nurse said, setting a brisk pace across the ranges in the fading light.

And how the good doctor loved our sleepy village. It was his destiny, against the odds, to escape across oceans, continents and mountains and find this ignorant little valley hidden away.

The established residents were a pompous, bigoted bunch easily swayed by a show of culture. In the parlours of the best homes Doctor Cameron played the piano and sang; recited favourite old poems from beginning to end; gave money to the right causes and showed a healthy disdain for all heathens, orientals and the local savages. The established residents accepted him on face value. Simple enough.

And the new immigrants had been blown from the European war, scattered in the blast, shot like pigs from a gun. Run, run to the farthest corners of the earth. Yes, they were well frightened. They did not want to be singled out. They knew the consequences. And, anyway, they respected the medical profession. Doctors were gods. The new immigrants would keep their heads down and their mouths shut.

But those halcyon days were numbered.

At precisely 3:45 PM the chainsaws stopped. Union rules. The men were quick to load the tools and the village trucks fled the street like pigeons winging homeward. The street was silent as a tomb.

The crew had cut the trees on Main Street from the lakeshore almost to the centre of our village.

Aphid and Priscilla were sitting on a stump at the place where the cutting had stopped. The stark line was drawn. Behind them, across the tracks and up the hill, the big maple trees still spread into green canopied avenues. Before them, descending to the lake shore, dreadful stumps. No sweet shade.

At this point of time, and in this place, sat Aphid and Priscilla, eating stolen camembert cheese and drinking stolen wine.

Horace rounded the corner at the bottom of Main Street. He carried a new batch of pamphlets for every door in the village. The pamphlets proclaimed,

"Law and Order Needed"

"Criminals At Large" and, finally,

"WHERE'S MY LEG?" A rhetorical question in large print.

Horace saw Aphid. His heart stopped. "You leg-thieving bastard!" he cried and threw his pamphlets to the ground and bounded across the barren wasteland of stumps toward Aphid.

But the street seemed so very long with no big trees to bounce off. The sound of his one foot striking the ground echoed from the barren walls. His rhythm was disturbed, he stumbled and by the time he reached the second block of stumps he was all puffed out and leaned against a lamp post to catch his breath.

Aphid and Priscilla sat on their stump drinking wine and watching Horace jump toward them. When Horace finally arrived he was too tired to kill Aphid.

"What has happened to the trees?" Horace wheezed and sat on the stump to catch his breath. Priscilla said,

"We can never understand," and she shook her head back and forth emphatically and passed the wine to Horace.

"Have some camembert cheese?" Aphid offered to Horace. The piece of cheese was huge, round as a wheel, thick and creamy.

"Thank you," Horace replied.

Aphid had stolen loaves of French bread to go with the cheese. Stolen tomatoes and dijon mustard and garlic pickles in gallon jars. Stolen butter and garlic sausage in big coils. Horace ate like a starving man and then Aphid said, in that solemn, nasal voice, "Horace, your leg is being used for a higher purpose, please don't be angry."

"Of course not," Horace replied, softened by the wine and he swigged a swig from the gallon jug and smiled.

The three of them sat on the stump and surveyed the dismal naked street and shared the wine and cheese like old friends.

"A picnic," Aphid said, and raised his hopeful glass to the barren sky.

✦ ✦ ✦

Aphid's picnic lasted all night long. Horace got drunk for the first time. Not his fault. He cried and cried as the memories flooded over him.

He was just a little boy with a wart on the bottom of his foot. His parents took him to see the good doctor.

"We must operate immediately," the doctor said, "because of the danger of infection." After that he remembers nothing until a dull waking. Slow grey dawn and his leg is missing. No leg. His lovely leg is gone. Where?

"A necessary precaution against further infection," Doctor Cameron sang like honey into their ears. Horace's mother and father, sweaty hands clasped together, fresh from the dropping bombs of Europe, listened. They still flinched at loud noises, lay stiff in their beds at night waiting for the footsteps. They knew better than to expect good news. They resigned themselves to one more torture and went home with secondhand crutches for solace.

"That is all he gave us," Horace sobbed upon the stump, "one pair of used crutches. Where did he take my pretty leg?" he moaned.

"What shameful grafting, what horrid purpose? Or, worse still, was there no purpose at all but hatred? Pure and simple hatred?" The sobs came up in gasps and his shoulders shook. Aphid and Priscilla listened and stroked his head. What could they do?

Then Bear turned up, wandering aimless down the empty street playing his lonely harp. And the other members of The Lymph Nodes staggered out of the Coldwater Hotel where they had been playing pool and drinking beer. From every direction the wild ones began to arrive.

Maybe they heard the chainsaws cutting through the gentle cooing of springtime. Maybe they heard the plaintive cries of Aphid and Priscilla running down Main Street.

Maybe they heard the first shy chords of music blown by the spring breezes. Maybe they heard the silence of death that surrounded all the other sounds and choked them out. Maybe they heard the bulldozers pushing through the mountains toward them. Maybe they felt the noose closing around their little world. Nobody knows.

Nature Boy came wandering down from his cave, brown as a berry, legs like pistons from miles of running. He wore a sleeveless wool sweater, short pants and wool socks tucked inside rubber boots that were cut off at the ankle and laced with binder twine. He ran miles in those primitive shoes, shuffling along very quickly. He lived on the high plateau to the west in winter and came down into the valley to pick fruit in the orchards in autumn. Toothless and wise, he loved to chat by the roadside.

In his youth, he had played his grand piano on top of the mountain in his little shack. The music flooded out of the windows and doors and across the mountain meadows and over the glaciers. Night after night he played and played to the mountain and the sky. But he was a squatter on the land and they burned him out and he went wild and ran and ran from his burning piano and never stopped. Without his piano he didn't know what else to do. His hands lay useless in his lap. So he ran and ran.

And then Wee Willie, the dog boy, crawled out from under his porch, tail between his legs, and sniffed the air nervously: something was different and dangerous and alluring. He pissed three times and slunk down the hill, staying in the shadows. He would never be caught, never again.

Alfie, born with no ears, came stamping his little feet up the street. That was how Alfie knew where he was: by the echo. Alfie felt the vibrations of the chainsaws through the ground. Felt the thud of trees falling through the soles of his feet. Alfie with no ears. Stamp stamp he went with his left foot all around town. When he reached the lower end of Main Street he went stamp stamp on the ground and the echo was hollow. The vibration was sharp. Then he saw the missing trees. He did not want to stamp his foot anymore. The feel was no good. He lost his confidence and stood stock-still until Rosie took his arm and led him up the street to the picnic.

And Rosie came down from her opulent prison in upper town, nonchalant, as if she were free every day. She wore layer upon layer of clothing and, as she walked, she disrobed, but under every layer of clothing was another layer of clothing. The strip show never ended and nobody knows the naked shape of Rosie. She danced and danced all by herself.

And so the party began. And in the middle was Aphid on the stump. And Horace, beside him, with his stump. And Priscilla, like a firefly, dancing around the stumps.

Even the animals came to Aphid's picnic. You remember my dogs and goats and ducks and geese, all quiet as clams while Aphid stole my lumber? Quiet as clams, do you recall? And the Mayor's Doberman dogs? Trained to kill they were. No match for Aphid. They rolled over, bellies to the sky, and whined to be scratched on their tender pink tummies while Aphid stole at leisure from the Mayor's backyard. Do you recall?

The animals came. The cats mewed and arched their backs against Aphid's legs. The meanest dogs sat docile, ears cocked. The street was lined with strays, mangy cats from the back alleys, not such bad characters, really, just down on their luck. Little pigs escaped from their pens (dug under the wire, crawled over the fence) and they ran about the street eating and shitting and squealing when stepped on.

And the children sneaked out from stuffy attic rooms, washed and scrubbed and ready for bed, wearing only pajamas. They crawled down drainpipes and sat quietly in the shadow of the sidestreets or in the cradle of a maple tree. They were drawn to an event they could in no way understand, but must must must see, hear, touch before the angry mother came grabbing their ears and, "Back to your bed," she says and, "Pray pray pray," she says. "You bad child," she says, "Those people are nasty, dirty, barely human," she says. Slap slap she went upon the bare bottom.

Only the orphans could stay behind into the late night. Nobody grabbed their ears. "She can't grab my ears, I don't have ears," Alfie mouthed and he mimed the angry mother trying in vain to drag an earless Alfie home. Everyone laughed. "Good Show," they cheered and clapped and Alfie lay his head on the ground, to feel the vibration, and went to sleep. Rosie covered him with a coat.

Constable Duncan showed up at 11 PM. City Ordinances. No permits. Noise bylaws. Litter. Unlawful Assembly. Public drunkenness. And drinking, drinking, drinking. Certainly marijuana. Maybe worse. Constable Duncan wrote the tickets. Scribble scribble pages and pages.

"Yes, yes," Aphid said to Constable Duncan, "All true, every page. But lookit the poor orphans all up and down the street. Lookit them. These are Doctor Cameron's children, every single one."

And Constable Duncan looked down the street at the

gathering of the town secrets. He looked for a long while. The street was silent. Hush hush. The constable turned his head and stared at Aphid. Aphid, disfigured because of that dreadful nosepicking habit. But why poor Aphid? Why only him? Everyone picks their nose when driving, don't they? He saw the people every day, driving and picking, picking and driving. Why should Aphid pay the ultimate price?

Then he looked at Priscilla. She had been butter in Doctor Cameron's hands. What was her crime? Dreaming of lilacs and youth perhaps? Being too short to see over the dashboard? Singing flat and loud?

And Horace, poor miserable wretch, why him? Immigrant parents? Easy prey?

And the mutant orphans all up and down the street, peering out and sneaking closer. Why them? Because they were wayward sperm in unwanted wombs? Spawn from shameful lust in barns and backseats? Fate? Karma?

Constable Duncan, like a true Military Man, turned on his heels and marched away. Click click click his heels disappeared into the distance. The trees absorbed the sound. He was tired of his slovenly wife and he was tired of the Mayor (who was fucking his wife). He was tired of all the churches vying for souls. He was tired of the sleeping citizens, cozy in their beds, while madness gathered on the street. He was tired of standing between the devil and the deep blue sea.

He turned his back on the town and over the hill he went. Not one glance back. No pillar of salt was he.

"Let the chips fall where they may," he said to himself. "Blind Justice. No justice at all. Justice be damned." He would learn to dance. Play the piano. Sleep late.

And our little village floated like a bubble on the waters of oblivion. The only law had fled. We didn't know we were a bubble ready to burst. We thought we were forever. If we thought at all. Now it is easy to see the inevitable outcome but in those days we were oblivious. We knew nothing else but our village. We were as ignorant as ants beneath a descending shoe.

✦ ✦ ✦

At 3 AM Aphid's forefinger twitched. His head rolled back his eyes glazed over his lips quivered and spittle ran down his chin. At 3 AM the last storm of spring rustled leaves on the sidestreets and, waking to her purpose, swirled down Main Street.

The last storm of spring was delighted with the missing trees. She picked up speed like never before. She used the barren street as a runway and took off in marvelous loop-de-loops, achieving heights and speeds she did not believe possible. She rose thousands of feet above the ground. Down she came into the streets rolling the garbage cans and breaking windows. With no trees to absorb her power she grew and grew.

Everyone ran for cover. Priscilla was scared witless and hid in the thickest trees she could find. Under the hedges, under the bushes, under she went, deeper and deeper. Finally burrowing beneath the spruce trees that covered the hill in Memorial Park, "safe, safe, safe," she sighed. The animals scattered and became eyes in the wall. The orphans ran beneath the bridge, where they always slept, and Horace bounded up the hill to home.

Finally they all were fled and Aphid sat alone upon his stump, feeling no reason to move. Before him, toward the lake, a barren street of stumps. Behind him, across the tracks and up the hill, lush avenues of waving branches: the cozy, verdant cloister of whispering trees.

And so the picnic ended. And this is how I came upon that scene in that late hour on that stormy night.

✦ ✦ ✦

I always loved the storms of spring and often walked the night till dawn and let the wind beat against my body and the rain soak me to the skin. The wind rattling the dark windowpanes in the old wooden frames wakened me from my slumber. The rain pounding on the roof disturbed me and forced me from beneath the warm covers. The thought of the cold wet earth unsettled me and I could not resist the terrible night. I rose and walked into the storms of spring again and again. I was wishing for lightning to strike close as kisses and drive my molecules wild. I yearned for a kind of death. Death to the common body. Death to the daily feed bag around my neck and the constant worries. And so I walked against the storm, into the open fields and down into the empty streets, longing for an electric transformation to set me free.

And that is how I came upon Aphid lying on his stump, with the barren street of stumps before him. The shaded street of giant trees rustling behind him. The howling she-wind around him.

When first I came into the street Aphid was prostate upon his stump. From the far end of the street he appeared lifeless but as I approached, through the roar of the wind and the flash of lightning, I could see his laboured breath. And closer still I could hear his sighs. And closer still I leaned over him and pulled back the lid of his one good eye.

"Sammy," he said, "I have been waiting for you."

"Is that so?" said I.

"Have some wine," he said.

"Thank you," said I and drank deeply. And so, first we met, face to face.

✦ ✦ ✦

"We must find Priscilla," Aphid shouted against the wind. We found her. She was burrowed beneath a spruce tree at the top of the hill in Centennial Park. She had several Orphans clinging to her for comfort and she herself clung savagely to the mammoth spruce trunk. We shook the Orphans loose from her with false promises.

"We will be back soon," we whispered into their sleepy ears.

"Soon soon," we sighed like the smell of wildflowers, covering them over with leaves so they wouldn't be cold. They stirred slightly but stayed sleeping.

We set off just as the dawn was creeping over the most distant hill. Aphid, Priscilla and I, walking briskly through the waving orchards in the magic light of the dawn. We found the boat hidden among the willows. We pushed off, using the oars as poles through the shallow water. The boat was leaking badly now. The poor old thing, all those sleepy years resting on the beach beside the packing house, drying in the summer sun, swelling in the autumn rain, splitting in the freeze of winter.

There was only one bailing can and Priscilla was in charge. To offer help would be an insult. She could handle the job. Aphid rowed and winked his one eye to me, as if to say, *humour her*. I said, "Ho Ho Ho away we go." But

APHID & THE SHADOW DRINKERS

I laughed alone.

Out of the shallows into the open water. Twenty feet past the shelter of the willows a blast hit our delicate bark. Shivered the rotten timbers. We all leaned left. We all leaned right, trying desperately to counterweight the wind. Aphid rowed, nonchalant as a count in a casino: confident his credit would be extended one more time. Priscilla, cheery and chatty, bailed oblivious with her little can.

Heavier and heavier the boat full of water. Slower and slower through the turbulent seas. My eyes darting about: the shore so distant. There was no turning back. Aphid and Priscilla were heading home. "Back to work," Aphid said, rowing vigorously through the choppy water.

There had been so much trauma in the village. The trees falling down was sad so sad. Then anger. Then stealing food and wine. Then too much wine. Then eulogies sung to the dead trees. Then manifestos of political action. Then more wine. Then Constable Duncan with his speechless speech. Then cheers and cheers when he disappeared, click click click over the hill and faraway. Then magic mushrooms in the wine. Then more wine.

Everyone told stories about the trees. Testimonials of first kisses beneath the private branches, willing lips. Memories of ancient fights beneath the trees. Spilled blood. Dirty kicks with sharp-pointed shoes. Broken jaws. Worse still, broken hearts. Unfaithful lovers discovered unaware in the tangle of branches: love in the shades. And songs were written and sung and forgotten and written again.

And in the midst of the festivities the last storm of spring blasted down Main Street and scattered everyone. Blew the empty gallon pickle jars down the empty street. The street, empty except for Aphid alone upon his stump and frothing at the mouth. And twitching through every muscle. Then limp as Raggedy Andy, apparently dead. Then speaking in tongues.

And now, out in the open water rowing against an erratic blast of winds, the magic mushrooms eaten with the cheese and wine began dancing inside every muscle fibre of Aphid's body. The mushrooms pumped up every cell in Aphid's body and he felt strong, like a superman, pulling against the raging water, challenging the storm. He felt the water and the wind inside himself.

Row like hell Aphid, I thought, but was afraid to say a word because a purple vein was popping in the middle of his forehead. He was performing like an athlete. His dip of oar was perfect in the rising and falling water. He swayed back and forth in perfect time to catch each wave and save us from a watery grave. His muscles were responding to some distant memory of youth and strength. The magic blood coursed through his veins. He was invincible. But for how long? How long could his frail body survive against the strain?

"Let me row," I implored but he was insistent.

"No no no," he wheezed and splash splash we were rocking wild in the wind. Priscilla was singing a sweet song, bailing demure as minuets, certain we would achieve the shore. Dip dip and swing across the water.

✦ ✦ ✦

I loved the sound of gravel grinding on that old wooden hull. Safe to shore we crawled. Aphid lay exhausted with the waves lapping his feet. Priscilla sang hymns and wandered through the woods picking herbs for tea. I, thankful, kissed the ground. We rested all day.

Then Aphid and I talked beneath the swaying lantern. I suppose you might think Aphid was too stupid, or confused or poisoned by the rotting finger in his brain to build a fantastic flying machine? Is that what you think? Most people did.

I am not a brilliant man and make no claims for myself. Every step of my crooked trail had been dogged by self-doubt. Nagging voices inside my head. So I had kept to myself and lived away from the busy streets. I had little success in the world of business. People felt uncomfortable in my company. And I felt uncomfortable with them. My life was of little consequence to the main flow of the village. I was a tolerated shadow. Because of my loneliness I rejoiced in every living being that happened into my small sphere. Animals traversing my yard, birds that nested near my house; those were my companions.

When Aphid stole the lumber from my yard I loved him for his audacity. It was a magic moment in the lonely pleasure of my day. As if a blue jay had stolen a whole pie from the window sill and flown to the roof top. As if stoats in vests had invaded the chicken coop and at this very moment sat about picking their sharp teeth with chicken bones.

✦ ✦ ✦

But now, Aphid, Priscilla and I are down the lake. Oh my god what have I done? Rowed into the drunken dawn with a madman at the oar. A little old woman, round as a berry, bailing water and singing hymns. I didn't mean to leave my warm bed so far behind. I thought I would be back by now, safe and warm, and congratulating myself on my audacity, my bravery, the way I had tempted the gods to strike.

"Strike me now," I had yelled into the night.

"Now with your mighty bolt, you impotent bastards."

And now I was badly stricken. Stranded on this other shore. A conscript to this abysmal work.

Most of the work, to build this Flying Machine, we could do ourselves. But the engines would require divine intervention, that was certain.

We woke early each morning. Priscilla cooking porridge and hymns. Stirring the big pot round and round, always under the tarp, of course. No sky for her. Aphid and I, discussing the intricate details of construction over boiled coffee. And our nights, sometimes to rest and sometimes off on expeditions to steal parts. Down the lake we went in the leaky boat just as the sun was setting. Aphid the insistent oarsman. Priscilla singing and bailing. Me gripping the gunnells, scared to death of the lapping water.

❖ ❖ ❖

We had few supporters in that miserable village. But there was the Greek. He made lots of money because his heart was so full of love that even the stingiest citizen wanted to reward him. He fed them in his little restaurant and the music was light dancing on water and the light was shadows dancing on the wall and for one brief moment the customers danced naked on a Mediterranean beach.

"More wine please, just a little," they pleaded. And they forgot their own names. "A little Ouzo?" the Greek offered. And they howled like dogs and screwed each other with joy and abandon. They yearned only to be connected to the earth. To roll in the dirt and to smell life. But really nothing happened and they went home. All a dream.

During the day the Greek dispensed floats and fountains and sodas and ice cream. And to the little children he always gave extra chocolate.

"So your heart will pump full of blood," he told them.

To the older children he dispensed wise advice,

"Don't worry so much. Just kiss each other and have fun; but don't get pregnant."

And at night he served a dinner of sensual dreams to the adult population.

We stole wine from the Greek. He made the wine in big oak barrels and we stole from him because we loved him. The wine wasn't very good but we never complained.

At first we were very cautious about our wine stealing. We stole only what we felt was absolutely necessary. We used a hose to siphon the wine into a jug. But soon we were drinking straight from the hose passing it around between us and soon we were sitting on the floor in the wine shed and the hose went back and forth and our jokes got louder and we snorted wine out our noses.

The Greek caught us. At first he was angry but eventually he saw the humour. Besides, he was tired from cooking up warm fantasies for cold people. People who forgot the beautiful dreams right away. They did not share the dreams with their neighbours as they should. In fact, they were scared someone might discover they had the dreams, so they hid them away. Husbands and wives, who shared the most intimate and delirious and sexual dreams, could remember nothing in the morning.

"What good is all my work if they just go back to that cold life?" the Greek moaned. "I must return to my native land before the warmth from inside my bones is eaten by these people. They cannot have the marrow of my bones. My flesh, my soul, my heart they may have, but not my bones." And soon we were all four sitting on the shed floor and drinking wine from the hose. The Greek was complaining,

"There are no Greek women in this village and I am lonely."

"Really," he continued, "this woman I dream of, she doesn't have to be Greek. But she must feel like a Greek and behave like a Greek and her blood must be very hot."

"And how should a Greek woman behave?" Aphid asked, roused from some deep meditation that had rendered him virtually comatose. "How?"

The Greek stumbled to his feet, planted his feet firmly apart, pulled up his shoulders, pushed his hair to one side. "She must behave like a Greek. I am the perfect Greek. And a Greek must have a bit of stomach. So this woman must be voluptuous." He patted his stomach to emphasis how good she would taste.

"This is because a Greek loves food. And to laugh. More than anything else to laugh and to love." Then he sat roughly back down as if the steam had gone right out of him and he sighed.

"But right now, in this place, there is not enough love to fill my heart. I need a woman to dispel these damp mists from my soul."

We staggered into the restaurant and the Greek cooked for us. The Greek had plenty of time, late at night, to eat and drink and talk about our situation. He wanted to help us because he could see we had problems. He didn't know about The Flying Project, that was still a secret, but he had experience with boats of all kinds and promised to plug the holes in our leaky rowboat. Priscilla danced to the Greek's music and played her castanets. She danced smoothly across the tile floor and shook her hair loose. Her hair was no longer blue but had gone wild and returned to its natural colour, a silvery gray. With her hair flowing down her shoulders, she was a mistress of seductive illusions moving through the smoky light of the empty restaurant.

At that moment, watching her disappear behind the potted plants, the Greek fell in love with Priscilla. "My god," he said, "This is the woman for me."

✦ ✦ ✦

Night after night we stole stuff. And with that stolen stuff we built vacuum systems and pumping systems and thrusting systems and rotating systems. Still it was no damn good. Too much weight and not enough power. We tore out all the stuffing from the stolen chair. We reduced the number of heavenly rolling bars. We used plastic instead of metal (a fatal error). Still not light enough. We shook our heads.

We needed divine intervention. Help From Above. And what did we get? We got the deep voice of the dead science fiction writer speaking clearly from beyond the grave. We trusted him. How could we not? He had come to Aphid spontaneously, from beyond the curtain of death, at a critical moment in our history. His sonorous voice had set Aphid upon the flying path searching for beauty. Or beauty and death. Or freedom. Or ecstasy. Do you recall? Beneath the maple trees on that fateful night the dead writer had spoken in a clear voice.

The dead science fiction writer spoke to us from the

Aphid & The Rocket Lawnchair

heart. His philosophy had compassion. He laughed at everyone: but gently. He was a humble man. His fiction, what little remained after The Great Fire, was full of terror and passion and the depths of all mans' black soul torn sentence by sentence from his flesh. He was a poet. Only his science was dangerously flawed. And how were we to know? Only his science was terribly flawed. This is how it went down.

Aphid's forefinger twitched inside his nose ever so slightly and I ran and fetched pen and paper. Aphid lay down upon the picnic table and the session began. "Hellooo, Hellooo" the handsome voice says, deep and soothing. Not Aphid's nasal monotone. No way. The beautiful voice says,

"Today I am sitting with Albert Einstein and we are in the seventh heaven for an afternoon picnic and Albert wants to explain a few things he forgot to mention when he was still alive."

Always the sessions began like this. Always with, "Hellooo, hellooo," and then some world-shattering message from some powerful dead person. How could we resist? This was not Aphid's voice. And the arcane texts, who could explain them?

This is how it went down. Aphid lay convulsing and frothing and thrashing on the picnic table and all the while his mangled left hand wandered calmly over a sheet of white paper and drew the pictures, intricate and beautiful, the measurements so precise. The lines as thin as hairs. The pencil held so strangely, because of the missing forefinger, between the thumb and third finger. And the wretched left hand so calm and gentle and perfect, like long dancing piano fingers, swept over the white pages and down came the notes, page after page, to build Our Musical Chair.

And so we built The Rocket Lawnchair guided by a deep voice from beyond the grave. And written down, stroke by stroke, by Aphid's mangled left hand. We had the blueprints. We had the instructions. We had the necessary ingredients (stolen, stolen, all stolen).

That damn dead writer. He meant well, I suppose. We believed him because he was dead and could talk through Aphid's nose in a handsome voice. I mean, what did Aphid know? Aphid was not capable of drawing. No way. Not in a million years. Aphid could not draw to save his life: not pretty drawings of horses in a field or architectural drawings or engineer drawings. Or any damn drawings. And he knew nothing about rocket science.

But there they were, page after page, "The Drawings". The lines perfect. The measurements precise. And all drawn freehand, and to perfect scale. Imagine that. And all drawn by Aphid, the clumsy oaf, barely capable of wiping his own arse with two hands. "The Drawings", rendered from every perspective, with cross-sections, details, annotations, footnotes, asterisks and references to recent and ancient scientific publications. "The Drawings", intricate and beautiful, were impressive for sure. How could we resist?

Down the first page, beside the very first drawing, in big simple letters, Aphid had written:

INSTRUCTIONS FOR BEGINNERS.
Step 1 – Assemble necessary materials
Step 2 – Acquire Permit For A Divine Intervention

And so we did. We assembled the materials night after

night. Then, in the broadest light of day, we marched straight to the Government Building, in the centre of our village, and we talked to the village clerk and we said we wanted to fill out the forms for "A Divine Intervention".

And, to our surprise, the clerk said, "fine, fine," and he stumbled off into the vault and was gone for a long while and he shuffled back out with the dusty file. He gave us the forms and we left. The next day we took the forms back, filled out neat as a pin, and the clerk took out his big stamp and bango, bango, bango in triplicate, in black India ink, we had the permit.

And so we acquired, with very little shuffle, a "Permit For A Divine Intervention". Yes, Yes, we most certainly did. It said so across the top of the form. It said, "PERMIT FOR A DIVINE INTERVENTION". Plain as day. In capital letters.

Why so easy to get such a permit? Who knows? Perhaps it was because this permit was so rarely requested, so there was no protocol to follow. And that will always confuse a public servant. Especially in our little valley.

Perhaps it was because the village clerk was old and about to retire and didn't want the hassle, didn't give a damn. He would soon be fishing. Perhaps it was because of the way we asked politely, please and thank you, with respect for the clerk's deep knowledge of the archives and the records and the rules. After all, he had outlived fifteen mayors. He put them in their place when they wanted changes, every single one. He told us so. And we listened and we nodded and we agreed.

And why would such a permit even exist? Did you ask? Did you wonder? A Permit For A Divine Intervention? How very strange.

You have only to consider the nature of our village to

understand how such a permit was necessary in the early years of settlement. All those religious zealots crammed together from every corner of the earth. Fleeing one after the other into our little valley until they were all mushed in tight together, surrounded by the wild woods teeming with its dark, heathen gods and painted savages. The old rules were smashed to pieces against this pagan rock. The fight was fierce to establish a righteous Christian God in this wilderness. So sect against sect wielded the sword of the lord, one against the other in a vicious contest. Those were dangerous times.

For one brief period, in the very early years, rival sects were claiming a divine intervention on a weekly basis, in order to outdo each other and win favour with the citizens. The divine interventions became more and more complicated, convoluted, and downright dangerous. Divine interventions became outlandish theatrical events, sometimes lasting for days and nights with much emotion and food. These religious events became disruptive to our community.

So a wise village council of that olden day ruled that a permit was required and a fee of twenty-five dollars must be paid for the privilege of entertaining "A Divine Intervention". In those days twenty-five dollars was a king's ransom. One year's wages for an honest man. Full payment on a small house in lower town. Not even the Catholics were willing to pay the fee. Soon Divine Interventions dwindled into legislated oblivion. Nobody could afford them.

But the statute remained on the books forgotten, until now. Until the dead science fiction writer whispered deeply through Aphid's nose and said,

"Go to the Village Hall and ask for The Permit. Ask for The Divine Permit."

And so we did. We paid our twenty-five bucks and we got The Permit and there was no stopping the project. We had our divine rights. We could build any damn way we pleased. We could steal at whim. Drink all night and work all day. The rules did not apply. A Divine Intervention has its own internal set of laws. Malleable laws according to circumstance. Laws changeable in an instant. At least that's the way we saw it. That is how we read the fine print of this archaic document dredged up from the dark ages of our village. And we read The Permit over and over. Every single Thee and Thou and Therefore.

"We are permitted," we shouted and we all laughed and we danced about the night fire until dawn.

"Do what thou wilt," Priscilla whispered softly just before she slipped into sleep.

"Do . what . thou . wilt," she said, dropping the words like four small, dark, stones in our path.

We did. We worked in earnest now. No fooling around. The party was over. At noon each day Aphid lay upon the table and went into a fit. Priscilla and I restrained him as he thrashed about quite violently. Aphid, in the trance, wrote upon the white page and drew the plans with the precision of an engineer and the delicacy of an artist and he frothed at the mouth and his eyes rolled back in his head.

This is how it was. His body in contortions, terrible spasms from head to foot, much dangerous thrashing and bleeding profusely from the left nostril. Except for the left hand. The mutilated left hand moving calmly over the pages. No twisting of the torso, no shaking no biting no spitting no screaming no begging no cursing can disturb the left hand. The left hand cannot be shaken from her task. That is how it was.

Then, when the fit had passed, Aphid lay worn out for hours, breathing heavily upon the table. Worn out from the psychic drain. Priscilla fanned him with branches and sprinkled water to his blistered lips. She tied bandages soaked in herbs to his bloody nose. She put cool compresses on his forehead and warm compresses on his feet. Late in the afternoon, up he groaned and back to work.

Back to work, building that infernal machine. The newest revision of "the drawings" crumpled in his fist; spread out on the table; pinned to a fir tree with a nail. And so we built the machine. We had help.

✦ ✦ ✦

From my notes: As usual, no date entered.

Inaugural Flight
Today we sent the stolen pig into space. The creature weighed two hundred and fifty pounds. She only weighed ten pounds the night Aphid stole her from the widow. We loved her dearly and regretted the lost bacon most intimately.

There have been several soul-searching nights discussing the merits of pork chops and whether it were not better to eat our little piggy grown large on roots from the forest floor. Our little piggy grown wild and obnoxious. But honour and duty finally prevailed and off she went into space, for the good of all mankind.

Things did not go well. The Rocket Lawnchair climbed

to a magnificent three hundred and fifty feet. Aphid intent at the ground controls. Then the thrusters failed to thrust. The secondary boosters did not boost. The pig descended rapidly. She landed splat in the lake: bacon after all. And pork chops in abundance. And roast upon a spit.

But we are sad this evening, with fat dripping from our chins. Poor little piggy. And such an abysmal failure for the project.

"More piggy please," said Aphid glum, very glum indeed. And Priscilla speared another pork chop from off the grill.

"Spiced to a T," she said all cheery. She was so very very thankful only the pig was dancing in heaven.

✦ ✦ ✦

We retrieved all the pieces we could from the lake. We rowed out and gathered them up. And we built again and we changed the rotators and we changed the thrusters and we stripped our baby down to skin. We ate pork. And Priscilla picked fresh greens and berries and dug roots from the forest to balance our diet.

No giving up now. New information needed. Aphid works harder. He devises welding techniques unknown to mankind. Cooks up super glue from pine pitch and piggy hooves in the porridge pot. Stinks to high heaven. Never sleeps.

The second model of the Rocket Lawnchair was beautiful. A melding of science and nature. The visionary and the practical. Blood Roots (Sanguinaria Canadensis) were soaked in a liquor to soften and then woven between the aluminum rolling bars to make a cage around the chair.

The cage was light and strong and flexible. The aluminum flashed in the light and the woven roots glowed cherry red.

Thrusters were lashed onto the sides of this cage. The thrusters were made from two alpenhorns stolen from the rooftop of the Swiss Methodist Church. The horns were twenty feet long, made of brass and weighed 300 pounds each. No job for amateurs, this stealing.

We practised block and tackle from the treetops and secret ninja chants around our camp, night after night. Three days of breathing exercises, sweat lodges, and walking on hot coals. And then splash splash down the lake we went in the dark of the moon.

Every Sunday the Swiss stood on the church roof dressed in their liederhosen and green alpen caps with feather. Every Sunday, at five in the morning, they stood on the church roof, steep as any alp, and blew those horns across the valley. They yodeled and slapped their heels with their hands and blew those godamned horns with no mercy at five o'clock in the morning. And they never fell from the steep roof to their deaths, as we hoped.

Out loud the village folk said,

"They have cloven hooves like mountain goats."

Behind their hands they whispered,

"Or the devil."

How else could the Swiss grip on that steep and slippery slate roof in the morning mist? Even way down the lake we heard those horns searching across the water. They scared us.

We took the alpenhorns home in the boat, of course, and a very dangerous task that was. One small breeze and we would be drowned. But, as you know, the breezes loved Aphid and not one breeze stirred a single ripple on the water. Even the north breezes, well known for mischief, held their breath. Two trips we made, one for each horn.

The horns were too long for our purpose so we cut them in half with a big hacksaw. A two-man hacksaw. We sawed and sawed that brass until our arms were sore. We slept. We sawed some more. Finally we finished. We stuffed the horns with pitch and lead as was written by the left hand, and spoken through the nose. We heated the horns till the pitch and lead melted and the brass softened and we twisted the horns round and round, precisely, according to the detailed drawings laid out by the left hand. We did what was written by the left hand. We did what was spoken deeply through the nose.

We attached the horns to the sides of the cage. Then we mounted controls on the arm of the chair so the horns could be adjusted to blow in any direction; down up sideways round and round. We hoped the horns would sound like the mooing of giant cows floating about in the sky. Melodious, but unusual and very deep. The alpenhorns, when pointing straight down, would push The Lawnchair up into the stratosphere and direct our musical flight.

The Lawnchair was mounted on a round metal plate. The chair rotated smoothly over the plate on thousands of ball bearings. Directly behind The Chair, in a severely vertical position, spun The Leg. The Legendary Leg Of Horace. The Leg spun on a small metal disk that spun on the large metal disk. All three spun on top of one another, each faster than the first: large disk then small disk then leg. A wheel within a wheel a'spinning way in the middle of the sky.

At the top of the leg, spinning around fastest of all, was the umbrella. The umbrella-propella. The incredible speed of all this spinning was made possible by no friction. No friction in the ball bearings, no friction on the big plate, no friction on the small plate, no friction at the bottom of the leg. No friction at the top of the leg where the umbrella-propella spun like greased lightning.

Why no friction? Do you remember the oils rubbed by Horace night after lonely night into that leg? Do you remember? They were the most expensive oils money could buy. Oils ordered from exotic places and sent by post from around the world. Horace was lonely and bitter and he had no other place to spend his money. And he had lots of money hidden in bundles throughout the house. And he loved his leg. And he hated his leg. And he rubbed and rubbed that leg with oils.

When the leg began to spin on the metal plates the oils warmed and when the oils warmed they flowed out of the pores of the wood and onto the metal plates. A continuous flow of the finest oils available to man, oils imported from Arabia and Mesopotamia and Egypt and the Congo. Oils from Siam and Japan and from the Arctic Eskimos. Oils from the Andes. Oils squeezed from plants that grew at the highest peaks and rendered one slippery drop for every million plants sacrificed. And oils from plants growing twenty leagues under the sea, compressed with the weight of water and released, into our atmosphere, through the wonders of modern science. Exotic oils from all over the earth covered every moving part of The Rocket Lawnchair. No friction. None. Greased lightning.

✦ ✦ ✦

"Oh well," Doctor Cameron sighed to his nurse, "I am old anyway. I have left my mark on the world, though I had

Aphid & The Rocket Lawnchair

hoped for more. We all did. Don't you remember, my darling? We had such ambitions." Never before had he called her "darling". Never. Not in all those years.

In their youth they loved only their work. Only the work. The wonderful work. The ruthless work of twisting fates. Freezing and thawing souls. Testing the limits of pain. But now they were old. Their bones were weak. The Doctor and The Nurse were sitting in lawnchairs outside the laboratory, enjoying the warm afternoon sun.

The laboratory was almost empty now. Most of the genetic experiments had escaped into the Wild Canadian Bush. Only the weakest were left inside the sealed rooms. "Life is full of disappointments," the nurse replied, "just remember the old days." And the doctor and the nurse drifted off into private reveries, their eyes rolling blissfully back into their skulls. They had left their mark on the world.

❖ ❖ ❖

"Come with me," Priscilla said to Aphid and she held him by the hand and led him to the big tub full of hot water that was sitting in the Saturday night meadow and she undressed him and washed him and Aphid smiled and laughed and kicked around like a child and spat water like a whale. "If you are going to fly you must be clean," she admonished. She scrubbed him all over and took his little penis in her hands and washed it gently.

I sat at the picnic table drinking dandelion wine and watched them play. They were so gentle with each other and Priscilla laid out a most dashing outfit of leathers and silk, "For you, my one-eyed friend," she said. And Aphid stood all naked in the meadow, shivering and oddly handsome, from this distance.

I was smoking hand-rolled cigarettes, Drum tobacco, one after the other. My nerves were so bad I smoked until I puked and then I smoked some more. This whole thing had gone too far.

There was no moon that night. The noise was very loud. Those big blades spinning around in the meadow and the oils in the leg were cold at first and wouldn't flow to the surface so the plates clattered, metal to metal. Aphid sat front and I sat back. Back to back we were and eyes looking out from all sides. Three eyes each way if we turned our heads at the same time. Or two eyes left and one eye right. Or one eye down and two eyes up. Both back and forth we had good control. Myself quite drunk on Priscilla's singing wine and scared shitless with all the noise. Loud noises have always made me jump. And water is deep and black. And ladders make me dizzy above the first rung.

I was the laughing matter when I was little. Barely able to walk up the church steps to Sunday school. Must hold fast to the railing and not let go and not look down. Never climb a tree. That was me.

"Little Samee Virtigo," the adults called me as a joke. "Scared of his own shadow," the children teased.

And I was. And I am.

But Aphid was having a great time, revving the musical engines. He was enraptured by the discordant clatter of metal and the primitive gushing forth of the first powerful notes. The notes resounded deeply over the meadow, almost too deep for the human ear. The sound emanated rhythmically from the Alpen Tubes, "Bu . . . Bu . . . Bu," like huge bubbles bursting, like the biggest tuba you could imagine blown by the softest lips, the saddest mouth. The sound was mournful, terrible and full of pain, like a mother crying for her dead child. The unbearable pain was all around us and Aphid and I cried and cried and I looked out through the swirling of blades and the mist of music and there was Priscilla standing naked in the field and the tears streaming down her face.

The engines were fuelled with symphonies. Beautiful music was fed into that terrible machine. All the great compositions were melted down and fed into the grinding jaws of the hoppers and from thence the music was drawn liquid into the twisted horns. The horns amplified and distorted the symphonies and a bastard sound blasted out like jet fuel.

And up we went. Up we went fueled by stolen symphonies. Our little ship began to hop across the meadow. Up ten feet and over ten feet and down with a thump banging roughly into gopher holes, wobbling up again with our thrusters blowing weird music in every direction. Finally up twenty feet in one single hop and over the treetops and Priscilla waving at the sky, throwing kisses, jumping up and down. Such a brave old girl, out in the open field all by herself, not even a hat upon her head. And so very small and round from way up here, waving, waving, jumping, crying.

◆ ◆ ◆

Worse than water, much worse, many times worse. Worse than a leaky rowboat in a sudden storm. Worse than the shore so distant, the water so cold and deep. Worse much worse to be up in the air in a wobbling machine, swinging over the wide water, the pretty little earth snug and warm below. Way below. Very much worse.

APHID & THE SHADOW DRINKERS

Aphid and I are back to back in a spinning disk with no head and no tail. And the blades are spinning way too fast. So fast they are only a whisper above our heads, the oils softened and flowing now, swoosh swoosh. And the thrusters mooing stolen symphonies beneath us and Aphid shouts, "I'm getting the hang of it," and down we go erratic corkscrew one hundred and fifty feet freefall almost into the treetops. We wobble up again and Aphid smiles a sheepish, "oops."

But steady at the helm off we go over the water and up the lake. Whisper of blades above and mooing of horns below, heading for the village in the dark before dawn. A raid.

This is the plan. We will shower pamphlets upon them in their dreams. And their dreams will be disturbed by the whirr of our alien ship. We will strike fear in their subconscious hearts and they will wake with a morbid taste in the very back of their mouths. They will open their doors in the early morning and the ground will be white with pamphlets. They will dimly recall strange dreams. Dreams of a wheel within a wheel a'spinning way in the middle of the air: just like in Ezekiel. Dreams of a Beast, with no head and no tail, just like in Apocalypse. Dreams of unearthly, unholy music spewing from this headless Beast, just like a trumpet heralding the end of the world. They will wake and be scared and read their bibles with their lips moving quickly and their finger on every line and they will think that God has sent an angel to warn them because they are such special white lambs on this dark, dismal planet: such good white lambs.

And because they are such good white lambs and because they fear the Lord God Almighty, they will cut no more trees on Main Street. And because they fear the Beast who heralds the end of the world, the citizens will sleep no more while Dr. Cameron works his dirty magic. That was our plan.

✦ ✦ ✦

Over the water in the early morning mist. Whisper above and moo below. Down we swoop upon the village. "Now" Aphid shouts and I throw the pamphlets. Up and over we go whirling in a big circle, swinging over the village and down again. "Now" Aphid shouts and white as snow they flutter down. And we are swooshing off and away; back whence we came, and landing smooth as lullabies for baby in the gushing dawn in our golden meadow. Home safe. Home free. The only perfect landing, ever.

Meanwhile back in the village. Good morning good morning a fine white Sunday. What have we here? White all over the yard and in the trees and still some last flakes fluttering down from way up high. Did you hear thunder? Did you see lightning? No, nothing at all.

"Snow in summer," shouts the widow lady across the pamphlet-strewn street to Horace. Horace, who dreamt all night his wooden leg was flying over the house and the leg was singing the most banal songs and little wings were attached to the leg and the little wings were beating frantically to keep aloft and the leg was surrounded on every side by many little beating hearts with beating wings. Beating wings and beating hearts were everywhere. And the air was filled with the sound of music. Insipid little ditties. Silly love songs. Teenage romance tunes.

And the widow appeared in every single dream.

Sometimes singing the love songs. Sometimes floating about in the sky with Horace's flying leg. The leg and the widow spun around and around in the sky. At one point the widow performed a cabaret number and her voice was sultry as smoke, her skirt slit to the thigh. All very disturbing and not Horace's style at all.

Horace woke and did his bounding exercises but he could not shake the awkward feelings. He went outside for his morning air and the first thing he heard was the widow shouting to him from across the street. Shouting about the snow falling in summer.

And farther up the winding hill in the uppermost part of upper town, a prisoner in her mansion, Rosie says, "Is it snow?" to her nurse and refuses to go for her morning walk in the walled garden.

"Is it snow, so cold on my toes?" Rosie asks and the nurse says,

"No, sshush now."

"Is it summer snow to wash away my sins?" Rosie asks again, suddenly happy, and then she rushes outside and gathers up armloads of the pamphlets. She reads them rapturously.

Each pamphlet is written by hand and each pamphlet is different. The scroll is either the beautiful oriental brushstrokes of Priscilla or the scrambled writing of Aphid or my writing, sometimes leaning bravely forward and sometimes leaning backwards to safety. Rosie clutches the pamphlets to her breast. She rolls in them and bathes in them on the lawn beneath the birdbath. "I am a white bird," she calls to her nurse who hauls her inside by the armpit. But she has the pamphlets hidden all over her body, in every crevice of her many-layered clothing. Rosie called the pamphlets, "Ten Thousand Flowers From Heaven".

And you, old church mother, what did you hear on that night?

"I woke to get a glass of water and heard a frightening sound. I heard death come knocking at the doorway. Bang bang and then I heard angels crying in distress, as if they were held captive. Defeated. Brought low. I went back to bed and slept a troubled sleep and heard the devil's music howling and the trapped angels moaning. The angels were forced to dance inside the devil's music like common prostitutes.

"I woke with a start from these dreams and opened the door and saw the pamphlets strewn about and read the first pamphlet and was shocked into a fit of cleaning and burning as quickly as possible these filthy little words will be gone. I swept the lawn and up my husband must go to the roof to sweep those pamphlets full of blasphemy away. He fell from the roof and broke his head open and the white pamphlets were stained with his blood. Then I knew this was the devil's work. And off I ran to my church to pray and ward off the evil that was floating down from the sky."

Good morning good morning.

❖ ❖ ❖

Starting Up The Machine

I will never forget the mournful sound of those first few notes, not as long as I live. The sound seemed to come from deep within the earth. It shook our innards so we almost soiled ourselves, and our muscles came unraveled in our bodies so we were unable to move. At first we laughed and then we cried. Oh we cried and cried for everything and nothing at all. The sound was like the birth of pain itself. All the pain the earth had ever known pulled up from deep and blowing out those horns. The Lawnchair tilted, rocking back and forth in the gusts of primitive music. And our sobbing became louder. And the primitive music tore at our bodies till we bled through our pores, until we cried blood from our eyes.

I guess I never really believed we would fly. I was ready to go home. To go home and feel sad and so what. To feed my geese and ducks and goats and dogs and laugh a little smugly inside about how foolish a person like me can be. From my lonely perch at the end of a muddy track on the outskirts of the village, after years of living alone, a person can get foolish and chase after silly things. This is because of loneliness and getting older and all kinds of subterranean reasons. But it happens. So I was ready to accept this and go home and not serve this evil god no more.

I never expected the pitch and pine tar the duggen roots the stolen chair the metal bits the twisted brass pipes the heavenly rolling bars the aluminum shroud the shiny spinning discs the ball bearings the leg the oils the hoppers the music grinders the umbrella-propella the symphonies blasting would ever get off the ground. To me, it was always a theoretical enterprise.

Not now though. Now we are whispering and mooing across the sky, not once but several times, back and forth in the early dawn when the people of the village are dreaming the most delicate dreams. When the souls of the sleeping people are wandering out across the land, freed from their fleshy bodies. When the souls of the sleeping people are free; that is the moment we must arrive. Timing is crucial. A moment too soon and the dreams are of poorly digested beef. A moment too late and the magic is fled into the dawn.

✦ ✦ ✦

There is a wind out of the south: big and round and hot. When the wind comes out of the south we know that spring is over. Finished. Now the heat is on us. But we are native sons and embrace the hot summer wind, revel in it.

Flying in the summer wind is the most lovely sensation. The wind is steady and strong and surrounds us and seems to buoy us lazily upward, like a big fat balloon. You would hardly know we had rockets blasting because we glide so smoothly across the sky. There is no possibility of a harsh landing. In fact, we cannot locate where earth ceases and sky begins. Blue goes on forever.

The symphonies of summer take on a different tone. They are sexual. And they float because of an intense internal pressure. They are ready to explode softly, disintegrate completely. There is no permanence in the heat. There is only a moment of longing and the moist sighs of string orchestras playing instruments of unknown origin; and then a dream of motion.

Aphid and I practise at night over the warm water. We swoop and climb steep on a crescendo. We never push too hard during an allegro. We coast and sleep through a denouement. And we dive to the earth when one thousand electric violins draw murderous clouds on the horizon and black lightning rocks the little ship. A poor choice of music can be disastrous in this valley, where summer storms move fast and dangerous across the open water.

Way up the lake, in the village, the sound of our engines is barely a whisper on the breezes. Our whisper above and moo below are lost beneath the noisy clutter of summer picnics and summer storms and summer fires and summer visitors from over the steep mountain passes. Summer visitors smelling of the ocean or of the plains. Smelling of long travel and dusty roads. Our whisper is not heard.

Aphid and I have flown on two missions now. I still close my eyes and feel my body dropping and spinning. Feel the chair a thin wafer beneath my arsehole and then all that space below sucking me down. The worst is when we stop and seem to just hang there swaying in the air, like an overripe cherry ready to split and fall. There is only a gentle humm, no real music at all. And there we swing gently back and forth, thousands of feet above the ground in Our Lawnchair. Only the music is holding us up and the music has stopped. Soon we will fall to our deaths.

And in my mind there is no end to the falling, even in death. The falling goes on forever. I am so dizzy I nearly fall out of The Chair. I puke into space and watch the bits of carrot, picked and eaten that morning from Priscilla's garden, fall away and disappear. Aphid tries to talk me down but he is no help. He does not understand the sick head feeling. The spinning space sucking me in, begging me to jump and die.

I did not believe we would fly. Never never never. Aphid was too fucked up with the rotting finger. And Priscilla? Gawd, she was hurt sooo bad. And me? I was scared of my own shadow. Scared of my shadow spreading over the town like a huge bat. Scared of my shadow, haunting me in the broadest light of day, like a dark mouth to swallow me up. You see, I am Doctor Cameron's firstborn son. I am his first child. Most loved and most despised. Egg of cold nurse and sperm of cruel man.

What hope had we?

◆ ◆ ◆

All summer long we flew and tinkered with the machinery. We consulted with The Divine Nose. The handsome voice became more and more difficult. The beautiful voice became rude and demanding. Abusive. "Hellooo, Hellooo," The Voice would say as usual, and then he starts in bitching.

"You stupid bastards are not gathering the material fast enough. You have no skills. You are clumsy. We need craftsmen and we get you. You are useless. Row harder. Sleep less. Build longer. Make less mistakes you stupid pieces of shit."

Even in anger the voice was as soothing as a hot bath and we yearned to obey. The voice said,

"If only *we* were still alive this machine would already be flying around the world. But you are stupid, stupid, stupid. If only *we* still had bodies. We, the glowing eternal minds of past and future geniuses from across the other side. We, The Divine Dead. Without us you are nothing. You are pig flesh and nothing more. Remember that little piggies. And remember what happens to little piggies that fly. Remember, we are the brilliant light guiding you."

He really gave us hell. But we loved The Voice, even when he spoke in divine anger. His was the righteous indignation of the gods. We believed.

And on and on The Voice demanded the absurd all

through the summer. And we obeyed, rowing this way and that, to gather the exact reed from shallow water or cone from ancient tree. Or pilfer the perfect linen bolt, or the ideal ink, from beneath the sleeping noses of the village. That dreadful music had hold of us, was driving us onward. That mesmeric voice. That insistent left hand.

◆ ◆ ◆

"Once a divine intervention has begun there is no way out. The participants must follow through. That is the rule."

Of course, we did not take *that* part of The Divine Permit seriously at all. We hardly even read *that* line. The Permit also said,

"There is no way out but through and through and through"

but that was section 36 paragraph 15 and particle 12 in very small print. We had drunk much wine by then, dancing about the fire. And we had no lawyer along to give us sober counsel. Or even drunken counsel. To inform us of the dangers. So we had signed. All three. In blood. One after the other we pricked our fingers and bled on The Permit: a single deadly drop under the moon light. We did so willingly and full of faith. We willed the heavens down to earth.

◆ ◆ ◆

Priscilla would not fly and could not fly and tremored in the thicket every time the blades began to spin and the horns began to blow. Counting her special beads. Singing softly for safe return.

Each time we started up those blades they gave up a dreadful moan. The horns below inhaled the mud and muck and rock. They sucked up our history of blood. And when the sound below and the sound above met, they swirled in the air in front of our eyes and you could see the music mixing together, become almost solid, take on forms.

And then history mocked us and every horrific act known to man began to dance before our eyes. And we saw ourselves throughout the centuries, changing costumes seamlessly with the music, changing bodies. And we were killing and raping or being killed and raped and the cries of pain and desolation and hopelessness resonated through our ship and we must follow wherever the music led us and we had no choice. That brutal life. Every club that fell on a gentle skull, we felt the thud, we swung the club. That brutal life buried beneath our foot. That dark music, soaked in the earth, drawn up into the horns by the spinning blades. We named this painful event, "Charging the batteries," or sometimes, "Filling the horns of plenty." Plenty of pain.

Then the horns, filled to the brim with our savage history, began to blow. The sound they made was almost below human hearing. And the painful moan of the blades, spinning faster now above our heads, was almost above human hearing. And our bodies were stretched between the high and the low. Our molecules were rearranged. We were destroyed by sound. Our bodies were broken down.

We had no eyes to blink. No head to turn away. We could not tell whether we spun or the blades spun or the visions spun. We only knew that we must cry and cry to see this bloody human dance. And finally finally our little ship would hop. And one single joyous note would play. Almost a wish. And then soon another and another and each happy note would hop us across the meadow until finally we are up and over the treetops and into the sky and the music is changed from dismal dirge of dying to howling, sadsweet determination, hopeful heart trembling beneath a loving canopy of whispering blades.

Then began a dark time of false prophecies in our village. The bells resounded up and down Church Street. The organs wheezed and the choirs chimed. The preachers prophesied. The ministers spake serious and low to the parishioners. The Roman priests, in their beautiful hats, waved the holy incense in clouds. Business was good. There was much to say about the evil thoughts that were floating down from the sky. White as snow on the outside but inside filled with the black ink of pernicious thinking. Even the Council of Holy Churches, meeting for the first time in village memory, put aside their differences and spoke in a unified voice. Never before, never again. They laid down an edict. The edict was pinned on every church door. Every single one.

So Sayeth The Holy Council, So Say We All:
Beware, lest you be tempted and driven into a desert of madness. Close off those orifices that offend. Especially, in these perilous times, close off the nose. Have nothing to do with smell. Breathe; but do not think of the nose. The lungs are for breathing; they are the engine for life. The nose is nothing by comparison. A mere appendage. Think not therefore of the nose. The nose has become a perverted thing

and is full of pestilence. So sayeth we all. Amen.

Wise council, under the circumstances.

✦ ✦ ✦

The Time of False Prophesies
We sneaked into the village and lay in the tall grasses and hid behind the trees outside the churches and listened to the sermons spewing hellfire like gasoline torches through the summer grasses. There would be no mercy for us. Our faces were scorched.

Every religious sect in the village was appalled, horrified even. "Blasphemy," they all cried. There were myriad sermons in the myriad churches. "God will punish such arrogance," they exhorted from the pulpit. "He has stolen from us," they wagged their hoaryheads, "every single piece." And it was true. Aphid had stolen every single piece.

The pulpits were full of terrible pronouncements concerning the fate of Aphid. As if a pestilence had not already descended on him. As if Aphid's forehead were not already marked with a sign. As if.

During this terrible time even the winds forsook Aphid. They turned nasty and spat at us when we flew. Knocked us about. Chopped us and dropped us and spun us and damn near flipped us and tore our shrouding and caused friction in the main bearings. Those capricious breezes. Even Aphid was scared. Forsaken in his time of need.

The summer had come and gone and the Autumn winds had no allegiance to anyone. Aphid was brave and stupid beyond belief. A disgusting figure now, haemorrhaging often and without warning. The disease had spread and he was degenerating rapidly. He smelled bad and not even Priscilla could keep him clean.

But he was strong as ever. Capable of feats of amazing strength. Holding the controls against all odds at very high altitudes. Working for days and nights welding and mending and preparing for the next flight. Polishing every panel; rubbing with precious oils, donated by Horace, every joint and socket. He cannot tell sleep from wake. The work is like a dream to him and living is no longer living but only dreaming of living. And drinking, of course, whatever he could steal.

In the local press they now called him, "The Monster Child".

✦ ✦ ✦

We knew they would come for us. They always do . . . sooner or later they always come.

They came down the lake with motorboats through the mists. We heard them the moment they left the shore.

"Six boats," said Aphid, "three fast three slow. Six Holy Men in each boat. Six times six and the battle begins." Thus spoke Aphid directly from his nose. His lips did not move.

Up we went to battle stations running into the pea soup mist. My head pounding from too many cups of stolen wine. I am sick and not ready for battle on this damp and cold morning.

Aphid is ready. Aphid shakes me hard awake and shakes poor Priscilla. Up we stumble and run, run to our pretty ship. And our little ship is pulsing warm and glowing darkly red beneath her canvas cover. Her batteries of liquid pain are supercharged. She has drunk her fill. She is impatient for flight. One scorching blast from the horns and we are catapulted into space.

Ugly wet morning. Damp and grey and cold. I did not want to move from beneath the layers and layers of blanket. I did not want to be way up in the air. Too fast too bumpy. Too many things can go wrong.

❖ ❖ ❖

Dr. Cameron knew we were flying. He had his spies, nasty little mutants still tied to his apron strings, still relying on his favours. And Dr. Cameron did not sleep at night. Not ever, not at all, not even with one eye open. He lay on his back and stared with both eyes to the ceiling or he wandered about the countryside on his midnight walks. Like father like son, they say. We both wander at night.

Dr. Cameron had not slept since before the war when he was a student, an apprentice in the laboratory. Few of them ever slept, those merchants of death. Sleep is too close to death, they knew too well.

So he was awake and he saw our ship and heard our ship and watched us from the top of Black Rock Hill as we swooped over the village. He ran down the hill in the dark before dawn and scooped our pamphlets and read them in the lamplight. And he was waiting.

❖ ❖ ❖

I feel that we are friends by now, if you have suffered through these tormented pages. And we have shared this odd history, you and I. This shadow history of our village, of our little valley. Now, you know more than most.

Because most that knew are dead. And those still living have lost their memories, or lost their voice, or lost their will, or they are simply lost.

✦ ✦ ✦

We flew right over their heads in the mist, those thirty-six priests and preachers and ministers. They heard a whoosh. They felt a deep shiver of cold through their spines. They heard a devilish drone. That was us, dancing on their graves.

By the time they arrived on our rocky shore there was only Priscilla dancing lovely and naked ahead of them, disappearing in and out of the cold mist like a sybaritic wood nymph. Her loose breasts promising warm milk to suck. A deep well of warmth between her ample thighs, a place for drowning, giving up giving in. A sinful return to innocence.

The sound of our ship in the mists had already shaken those Religious Leaders and the sight of Priscilla dancing naked on that cold and lonely shore unnerved them and they clambered frantically up the trail in all their various finery.

Our camp was burning, the smoke was rising, this bird had flown her coop.

✦ ✦ ✦

"More rhythm," Aphid shouts from front and I shout, "strings more strings," from back and up we float and turn and twist as if we knew the whole damn song from beginning to end. We climb gentle as cooing tropical birds up through the fog and into the clear blue sky above. This is most fun and even I feel safe and secure skimming o'er the fluffy cloud tops. I am not sick.

❖ ❖ ❖

The Rocket Lawnchair was better going up than coming down. Much better. Going up she was as smooth as mantras sung by a thousand pure-hearted monks. Beneath us the engines sang deep and hollow and full of longing. Above us the blades spun soprano operas sung by Divas of the high notes, above us thousands of musical insects rubbed their wings as fast as light, sparks flew and tiny fiddles and flutes harmonized the highest notes gently out of hearing. That was The Rocket Lawnchair climbing. Up she went in a whisper and a roar.

We should never have flown on that dank day. Now we are lost above the clouds and no way to tell where we are. Up here, above the clouds, is beautiful and blue like heaven. We are floating with no bearings on our compass, no earthly anchor. We turn our heads and wave to each other. Aphid's face is round like a moon against the clear blue sky and grinning from ear to ear. We have made our great escape. But there is no way down. The clouds are thick as wool beneath us and we have no instruments of detection.

But Floating, that is best of all and our only just reward. Floating is no one thing, it is a combination to unlock. Machine and mind and soul and spirit and body all smooth together, like rings thrown up in the air. Floating is timeless. Floating is time most perfect. When floating, the heart must swing like a pendulum with a joy for dying in every stroke and the heart must whisper as it swings, "Just one more stroke before I die." Otherwise there is no Floating.

And Floating is a fleeting mistress. Pretty and fickle. A

coquette of the very worst kind. She has stolen you up and away and now you are a flickering chimaera thousands of feet above the hard ground. You do not feel the danger. You do not see the danger. You are empty. You are cloud. You are wind. You are motion. You are full.

> You give your life away
> for one sweet swing over the moon,
> one cat one fiddle one silver spoon.

But when this mistress leaves, you cannot remember her face or her name or where you met her or why she left. You only remember a feeling. She is an enigma, a riddle you solved just once. And when she leaves . . . but coming down . . . that is another matter.

✦ ✦ ✦

And coming down, even on the clearest day, our little ship was short and squat. She had bad hips. She didn't do stairs so good anymore. Coming down she was no prom queen dancing. Her blades were neurotic and difficult to control. They wobbled and stalled. Her engines farted. Her music faltered.

We had practised all summer to make our landings smooth but coming down was always rough. Our eyes were damaged by too much seeing in the thin atmosphere, so we were half-blind. Our skin was burned, underneath our clothes, so the touch of our clothes was a torture of needles. And down we came with a thud in the meadow, breaking precious pieces. Bouncing graceless across the gopher holes.

But now there is no way down and up we cannot stay.

We do not belong in heaven. The music of the spheres cannot sustain us; it is too pure too sweet too close to God. We need a music full of blood to feed this damned machine. Bloody human music. The imperfection of human souls played endlessly on a string.

Aphid gives "thumbs down" and we drop into the clouds. We fall and fall peering out from every side to catch a glimpse of cliff or hill or any solid thing. Soon we are completely lost inside the clouds. Maybe we are descending gently? Or maybe we are plummeting straight to earth like a wingless goose?

People should not build ridiculous machines. And people should not ride in those machines that they should not build. Especially in the fog. We are soaking wet and steaming cold and we cannot see through the glass. We are blind and falling and shivering. We are searching for land.

✦ ✦ ✦

Dr. Cameron knew the hour of our arrival.

His cannon was ready to blow us from the sky. His snares well devised. His nets stretched out to catch us like a butterfly. The faithful nurse was always at his side.

This was their swan song, a duet. The two of them together again, singing anthems. She, once again, carrying sandbags to shore up the trenches, bringing sandwiches for the troops. He, young again, whispering orders, developing weapons late into the night.

And His troops? They are my little brothers and sisters, the ones we left behind in the cells. The ones that could not leave or would not leave. The favourite ones. The pampered ones. They care for nothing as long as their food is slipped under the door at night call. They do feel for the other cells. We tap on the walls and they do not reply. They are well fed and we are hungry. They obey. We spit. My little brothers and sisters, they will do anything for She and He. Our Mother and Father. Oh well.

And our troops? Our loyal troops? Where the hell are they? We pray they are running now to scale the cliff and silence the guns.

The clouds parted and the village appeared beneath us. The church spires right below our feet. "Oh wonderful," Aphid cried, renewed in spirit, "I can see the common green." We did a double loop-de-loop and made the engines sing. Woke the sleepers with a start. We didn't care. Our cover was blown, our camp was burning and we had no place to go. "Fuck 'em all," Aphid shouted above the music's roar.

All the nasty siblings on the clifftop running now to battle stations. But our army is nowhere to be seen. Maybe they did not understand the messages encoded in the floating pamphlets? Maybe they didn't read the pamphlets at all? Maybe they got drunk last night and slept late? Maybe they didn't give a damn, had given up the fight? Maybe they were scared of dying? Maybe they were scared to kill their own father? I was.

We flew above Main Street. The tree cutting had continued over the summer and whole blocks of trees were gone. The work had only stopped because the mayor had drained all the money and run to South America. They always did in our little valley. Time after time.

Priscilla had stolen all six boats and left those thirty-six religious leaders stranded on our distant shore. She wrapped her naked body in stolen holy cloaks and towed the boats behind her. "I am Little Bo Peep and these are my sheep," she sang to herself out in the open water, and she wagged her tail of boats through the waves. She still feared the sky and wore big brimmed hats and kept her eyes straight ahead and did not look up. She chewed her lip till it bled.

Priscilla arrived in the village ahead of us for we were lost above the clouds, Floating, for quite some time.

◆ ◆ ◆

There is no army running to our rescue. No saving grace of unified madness. Shit no. Only Priscilla, sneaking from tree to tree, ready to die for love. And dog boy pissing himself, ready to kill for hate, yearning to bite the hand that fed him. The orphans do not care, they are busy looking for food and shelter, fending for themselves, as always. And who can blame them? And Alfie is scared stiff, no good to us at all. He is catatonic. Too many bad vibrations.

Horace, however, is well equipped for battle. He is bounding up the mountain in mail-order army fatigues with mail-order bullets strapped in bands across his chest, a mail-order knife between his blackened teeth, commando style. He means business.

And Rosie has escaped and is running with white gown floating behind, ballet style. "I give my body to save the world," she sighs in a wavering falsetto. She is determined.

And on the clifftop, from our ship, we can see Dr. Cameron and his troops standing ready at their stations.

They fire the first shots.

We fly up the hill toward the cliff, straight into enemy fire. The bullets go "ping ping" into the fuselage. Aphid and I are laughing, devil-may-care. The small bullets are useless; they cannot penetrate our woven shell.

Dr. Cameron and his troops take their time. They set up the big gun. To them, we seem to be floundering up the hill. Maybe they should have another sandwich while they wait? the nurse suggests.

When Dr. Cameron looks down from the cliff he sees a butterfly flitting up the hillside. "Awkward and slow," he says to himself but he cannot take his eyes from her clumsy grace. His troops are loading the big gun . . . but their movements are slow and dreamy. They are moving in time with the butterfly. They do not know that The Lawnchair is deceptive when climbing. She is mercury, quicksilver, liquid speed. A wrinkle in time. But watching her you might say, "She doesn't know which way to go," you might think, "She doesn't know where to land." You might muse, "The wings are too big and floppy." Not so. The butterfly knows her nectar. Up we go.

One bite from the sandwich and we are over their heads. The big gun is not ready. The troops snap out of butterfly-dreamtime. They swing the gun to follow our erratic ascent. They fix us in their crosshairs and we slip left, slip down, become a rosy blur of sound. They fire once. The big shell whistles passed our ears.

✦ ✦ ✦

The citizens are wide awake now. They argue in the streets with each other and point to the sky. They do not like being wide awake. So many disturbing sensations racing through their bodies. The baby they forgot in the bathwater so many years ago. How could they have done such a thing? They are shocked at their own behaviour.

"But still, we had our reasons," they decide. And that is that.

All up and down the street people are remembering deeds long past, long buried, better forgotten. And all up and down the street they are denying that it was them that did those things.

"Never me," they say, "I was at church and had my head bowed down."

"T'was my vicious twin," they state with certainty.

And mostly they say, "Wasn't me, I was asleep with no dreams."

◆ ◆ ◆

And the citizens are angry with us because of the noise. They plug their ears with cotton balls: still we penetrate. Our sound is vile and disturbing. We are the Antichrist howling inside their bodies. They want to kill us. After all, they were so softly sleeping.

We are stuck together, them and us, with sticky black blood and golden straw and venomous white spit. We are stuck with a nasty glue.

◆ ◆ ◆

We hover a thousand feet above the clifftop fortress. Aphid yells to me "hold the controls," and stands up in The Rocket Lawnchair. Never done before, too dangerous. He unzips his many pants, pulls out his cock, and pisses and pisses and pisses. The pissing will never stop. His bladder is a bottomless reservoir. The Rocket Lawnchair, under my command, describes a lazy circle and the horns blow the piss into a maelstrom and the piss freezes in the cold, high atmosphere.

And a hail of piss stones rains down upon Dr. Cameron and The Nurse and our little brothers and sisters. When they look up to aim the big gun, a piss stone smacks them in the eye. Blinded, they shoot anyway. Again and again, wild shots.

Now we are directly overhead. They fire. I feel the shell leave the gun. I feel the shock of air hurling toward us. I feel the perfect shot, directly toward our tender underbelly. I jerk The Lawnchair to the right, an evasive maneuver, and Aphid falls out of the ship. Tumbles away with his cock in his hand and piss spraying down his pants and all around him in a frozen yellow mist and the big bullet thunders by so close I can feel the wind. We are not touched.

The bullet stalls above us. Turns and drops. And Aphid, precious Aphid, where is he? I cannot see him anywhere below. I look up and the bullet is falling straight in my face. I dodge left and Aphid is back on deck, standing by his chair, no longer pissing but his cock still in his hand.

"Floating," he says to me, "I was floating in the mixing musics, most perfect," and he winks his one good eye and smiles big showing rotten teeth.

"Most perfect," he repeats and plunks himself back in his chair.

The bullet whistles by us heading to earth and we look down and the shell lands with a thud on the big gun. There is a deadly quiet and then a "booom". And another and another as the neatly-stacked bullets explode and whizz around the hilltop. The fortress is destroyed and pieces of arms and legs and skulls and guts are strewn about and draped over the smoldering ruins. Then quiet, very quiet.

And through the smoking wreckage comes Dog-boy snuffling, chewing on a tender morsel, burying meat for later, rolling joyously in the gore, draping himself with intestines for a necklace, gall bladders hung from his ears like cherry earrings. Pissing on every single thing, claiming for his own. "Vengeance is mine," he howls.

After Dog-boy is finished his work, ripping the flesh to pieces in a rage, scattering the bones, burying all the pieces in a thousand secret places. After that, there is no way to identify the victims.

Dog-boy claimed he ate the Good Doctor's heart and gnawed at his skull, made a soup with his eyes, tongue and scrotum and left his brain for the crows to eat. "Sweet meat," he growled, "He tasted so good, I buried him in a special place and ate his rotting flesh for weeks." So says Dog-boy.

Rosie, hiding at the base of the hill, swears she saw The Doctor running hand in hand with The Nurse through the pine forest, after the explosions. "They looked like children," she said, "smooth skin and pink cheeks and strong limbs. They were running and laughing and kissing each other. Somehow they found me in my hiding place; they turned and looked at me and their eyes were yellow. They came over to me and I couldn't move and they cut me with a sharp finger and lapped my blood with their rough tongues." And Rosie showed me the slashes all over her body. "And inside too," she said. Her white dress was covered in blood and blood ran down her legs. So says Rosie.

So nobody knows for certain who lived and who died in a hail of frozen piss stones. And, if The Doctor and The

Nurse be dead, then what is death to them? Did they fall into the fiery lake? Will they suffer for eternity? Or is death naught but a door opening to a larger evil, for Daddy and Mommy? A promotion. More opportunity. A bigger clientele. Maybe yes maybe no. Nobody knows for certain.

And there is nothing left but broken concrete, on the clifftop, if you know where to look.

The citizens of our village, harassed by the ghosts of their victims, spilled into the streets. They cannot go back to sleep. There is no way back. That is the rule for a Divine Intervention. There is no way out but through and through and through.

And they cannot face the ghosts who appear as solid as flesh, and harangue them mercilessly with questions.

The ghosts have always been awake but their voices were muffled behind a curtain. And their bodies swayed like a curtain in the half-light. Not now. Now they take over the house. The little ghosts sleep in your bed between you and your wife.

"Why did you give me to Him?" the baby ghost whimpers all through the night. "I paid for your mistake. I had no sin of my own. Why was I tortured into this shape? Look at my limbs!" You cannot stand to look. You toss and turn and sleep is impossible.

"Why me?" cry the bigger ghosts, seated in a favourite chair close to the fire, "I only needed a rest. Some love. I was not completely lost. But you gave me to Doctor Cameron and The Nurse and They ate my damaged soul for breakfast; tore the good genes from the bad and left me without a name, without a history. They cut pieces from my double helix, from my coded core of self. They chopped them out like splicing film in a cheap movie and left me naked on a concrete floor. They carried the pieces away in tubes, across the laboratory. I watched them as I floated through the roof and died."

There was no escape from the ghosts; they were inside every home. And outside the howling of that infernal flying machine, the thud of the big shells into the hillside and the explosions from the clifftop were most unsettling.

And the leaders were all gone: Constable Duncan and The Church Fathers and The Mayor and The Doctor and The Nurse, all gone somewhere else.

There was only Priscilla standing on the steps of The Government Building, in the centre of our village.

✦ ✦ ✦

Little Sammy Virtigo never meant to go up in the air. Never meant to fly or even climb a gentle slope. Now look at me. Way up here all alone with Aphid. And look at Aphid, bleeding bad and his eyes rolling back. We are in big trouble now. Aphid is bleeding through every orifice in his head. Internal bleeding too, throughout his body. He is a dying man.

In the throes of death he has the strength of ten men and I am so very tired. The music is breaking up. The symphonies are no more. Now there is only industrial music with no audible lyrics, no melody: only the fascist beat of armies marching and the chant of angry voices beneath us in the streets.

"Down we go," Aphid says.

I say, "No, please no,"

He says, "What else?" and there is no else. There is only down. So down we go.

Once you forget your little life, Diving is most wonderful. But first you must forget your life. Sell it away to the lowest bidder in a flea market auction. Even your pendulum heart, so precious swinging, sell that cheapest of all. For a pittance. That is Diving. Diving is most beautiful of all. Most deadly.

Once you forget your little life you will be happy Diving; but first you must tear away from the loving snares. You are still attached to your pitiful life, so you do not fall with grace; you flail about. The faces of loved ones spin by and disappear behind you. You call to them but the words are stuffed back in your mouth by the wind. The blood rushes to your head, to your feet, to your head as you roll and plummet. The earth rises up to greet you, soft and green.

Now we are Diving and Diving is death.
Annihilation most complete.
Machine and mind and soul and spirit and body,
All rings on the pavement in a clattering heap.

Aphid has the controls in a death grip; he pushes the lever forward. There is no deep voice guiding us, no last-minute surgery to cure the flawed machine, no angelic devices to elevate the soul, no gentle visions of celestial beauty to coddle the spirit. Only wind and fear remain.

Below us Priscilla is swarmed by the crowd. They blame her for the invasion of ghosts. They blame her for the sleep that is lost. They blame her for the noise overhead. They shout insults and call her names. It is a mean crowd.

"It's your damn pagan chanting that has brought this upon us," they shout.

"Why couldn't you leave well enough alone?" they hiss and poor old Priscilla has no special root to cure their anger, no soothing cup of herbal tea. She never expected so much hatred. She never suspected they couldn't be calmed. Despite the fact that she had seduced all thirty-six religious leaders into leaving their boats and discarding their cloaks. Still, she never expected.

But on the Government Steps there were no morning mists to conjure a gentler version of the truth. She could not dance and disappear through the birches and the cedars. She could not hop across the slippery creek stones to hide amongst the roots under the sandy bank: her favourite spot. And on the Government Steps she could not hide behind her words; no one would listen; no one could hear.

So they pushed her and hit her with sticks and pulled at her hair and clawed at her clothes and spat in her face and pulled her down and stabbed a pitchfork through her throat. Simple.

And as Priscilla's blood began to flow, the citizens felt sleep returning to the village. One by one they fell asleep on the grassy hillside of the little park. Or they wandered back to their houses into a sleep with no dreams. They felt safe again. And the ghosts were, once again, only a murmur behind a curtain.

But sleep is not that simple and even spilled blood brings only fleeting peace.

✦ ✦ ✦

Nobody could save Priscilla. Neither Horace running to her rescue, loping down the hillside, firing his rifles into the air, howling for justice or mercy; nor Aphid diving to his death (and mine). Not even the Greek, who loved her and dreamed of holding her big warm body in his hairy arms, and would have laid down his life to save her. Nor the tough little orphans, who despised everyone, but clung to Priscilla's skirts. The orphans crawled between legs into the crowd, slipping their way to the front line to save Priscilla. But all they got for their trouble was Priscilla's blood splattered on their faces and a ghastly view, eye to eye.

She is killed too quick to save.

And the rest is written in the archives. You can read it for yourself. The way we fell like a spinning stone from the heavens. *Hallelujah*. The way our burning ship lit up the sky for hundreds of miles. *Praise the Lord*. The way the blades blew apart and sent a shower of fiery debris over the entire village, setting the rooftops ablaze. *Amen*.

The way the Swiss Horns exploded into a myth of diabolic new sound, melting the earth, boiling the waters, shattering the air.

The way The Rocket Lawnchair crashed through the roof of The Grande Hotel and the fireballs leaped up and exploded and the hotel burned to the ground so fast beer glasses were found melted in the hands of drinkers who were turned to cinder before they could twitch. Twixt the cup and the lip a terrible slip. But you can read it for yourself. You can look at the pictures. Just go to the archives.

The way the village burned and the people ran all night

with buckets and brigades, hoses and ladders. Fire fire everywhere. No sleep.

The way the sooty morning dawned and the citizens sat dazed and defeated on the rubble.

The way the bulldozers, pushing the new highways through from east and west, arrived that very morning and found the village razed, and the citizens ready to sell at any price.

✦ ✦ ✦

The way I was found, flung into the thicket and cut with hawthorn and rosethorn and delirious (as usual they say) and badly bruised and burned all over. They did not find me for several days. I was hanging in thorns all that time.

"Sammy," they said when they discovered me in the brambles,

"Why were you out walking in the storm? You trying to get yourself killed again? You little fool."

"You trying to get hit by lightning again?" they said and I opened my mouth to tell them where I had been and what I had seen but my tongue was thick and I couldn't find any words in my skull. The words had been turned to ashes.

There were two of them that found me, big guys, and they carried me to the doctor's house on top of Black Rock Hill and he cleaned my wounds and pulled the thorns from my flesh. The doctor told me,

"Go home, be good and stop trying to get killed by lightning."

"This time you almost did it," the nurse said as she bandaged me up, "I don't know how you survived." And the doctor prescribed a double dose of medicine.

I was badly burnt. The lightning bolt had gone up one

leg and down the other, like an angry ferret trapped in my pants. Damage was done.

"Stay at home," the doctor said, "Read the bible and count your blessings."

So I listened to The Good Doctor's advice and I stayed with my goats and ducks and dogs and geese for company and studied the bible cover to cover, every single word. I was hoping for salvation and wandered no more into the night looking for lightning bolts to strike as close as kisses and drive my molecules wild.

✦ ✦ ✦

I still see Horace hobbling about. He's not looking so good. He drinks too much and he can barely swing his stump over the bar stool. And if you ask him to tell you a story about the glory days when he was a warrior and a dancer and an athlete, the old days when he knew who he was, he might tell you. And he might not.

The rest of them are gone. I never see them. The Greek went home to Greece and I am certain he is warmer now and bathing naked on a beach with more friendly folk. And Nature Boy ran so far the hounds couldn't catch him. And the orphans grew into a life of crime and went to jail, of course.

And me? Sometimes children point and say,

He's the one got hit by lightning and went crazy.

And me? I stay close to home and take my medicine. Doctor's orders.

Epilogue

When you are a child, your life is the way it is. You are just there, plunked down on the grass at safety's feet, and off you go to see the sights. You accept everything as the way it is. You don't have the years of experience to see change, so everything has an immutable quality. The quality of a truth. A foundation to build a universe of your own. Granite blocks of precious memory. A gunny sack full of the secrets of the world. Everybody keeps giving you the secrets. They want to get rid of them because they have so many and they weigh so very much.

Our little town was ringed by madness, by anarchy, by a tinge of colour from a realm outside the common rules. The Rules of Order were a thin veneer stretched tighter and tighter over a cavern. Our little footsteps echoed on the earth as if it were a drum skin. The sounds reverberated in the huge belly of the drum, larger than life.

The drumming of our footsteps disturbed the slumber of The Large Dark Ones and they became dimly aware of our presence. Our little feet, making a big sound, on the taut skin of the earth. Our future was waking, dim and menacing. Unformed energy rising to meet us like dark steam through the dry cracked earth. The steam escapes and hisses a continual refrain through the velvet hills, "No promisesss. No promisssess" like the whistle of a night train disappearing.

But we danced the ordered circle of five o'clock suppers, oblivious as cows, and played kick-the-can into the dusk and dark, till the whistle blew us come home over the backyard fences. Sweet summer nights a blessing of cool. At home we were marched through our rituals, orchestrated by mother. The pajamas and the brushing and the washing. Marched through the stuffy attic bedroom to the attic porch where we slept behind the screen, high above the street, where the cool breezes blew all night long and the waving trees laid patterns across our beds, back-lit by the moon, and all pervaded by the smell of dust, dampened by warm summer rain. Outside there was thunder, lightning and big drops on the dusty ground. Under our beds the future lay coiled. Not asleep and not awake. But in some other state not yet discovered.

Years later, we would get lost in the world in our own way, our own time. We would become the wild ones, half-crazy with our own ideas, half-starved and driven by hunger pangs we could not possibly satisfy. We would drink the shadow. We would be the outsiders. We would be our own lost stars plummeting through space.

Perhaps we are flung into the bottomless pit and the fall is so eternal it feels like flying? For fleeting moments we ride the currents, the hot updrafts. For fleeting moments it feels like flying.

But today we are walking, my friend Pete and I, with the most pleasant breezes blowing and the range hills across the valley burnt to brown, even during this wet summer.

Printed in September 1999 by

in Longueuil, Quebec